MW01251612

Protect Me Not

She wanted to make peace with her past, he wanted revenge…

Protect Me Not

Written by Joanne Vivolo

This novel is fiction. Any names, characters, places, and incidents are products of the author's imagination and are used fictitiously. Any resemblance to any events, actions, locations or persons, living or dead is entirely coincidental.

Copyright © 2016 by Joanne Vivolo

All rights reserved. No part of this book may be reproduced or transmitted in any form or by any means, electronic or mechanical including photocopying, recording, or by any information storage system including the internet without the written permission of Joanne Vivolo, except where permitted by law.

ISBN-13: 978-1534735200

ISBN-10: 1534735208

ACKNOWLEDGEMENTS:

Domenico Vivolo: My husband I adore you. I have so much love and respect for you and all of your steady tolerance toward me during the good and bad times life bestows upon us.

Adele Cabral: The one I look up to, admire and try to emanate. You are my sister by blood, my best friend by choice. There is nothing in life we can't get through. Together we are that much stronger. Thank you for always walking beside me.

Darla Crisante: A sister is defined as a female sibling, but you are so much more than that to me. Finding the light at the end of every dark tunnel is a quality you exhibit so effortlessly. Thank you for shinning bright; to help guide the way through those dark tunnels.

Dianne Bissett: The Best Mother a girl could ever wish for. You have supported every one of my dreams, encouraged all of my aspirations and offered words of encouragement every step of the way. I am proud to be your daughter. Thank you.

My Children: Everyday you teach me fundamental life lessons. You are all my center of gravity. Together, you make me whole.

Dawn Sherwin: I knew from the moment we said hello many, many years ago that we would remain lifelong friends. You taught me the ins and outs of radio and what it was like to be the best at traffic scheduling. I'm thankful for your guidance and mentoring. Thank you for being that true friend that only a few select people are blessed enough to find.

Lea Black: Yes, you! Sometimes called the Mayor of Miami, you lead with elegant poise and sparkle of course. Thank you for empowering lives every day, mostly mine. Your dedication and help does not go unnoticed.

Often it's the deepest pain which empowers you to grow into your highest self...*Karen Salmansohn*

*

The key to change is to let go of fear...*Rosanne Cash*

*

There are far, far better things ahead than any we leave behind...*C.S. Lewis*

*

That, which does not kill me, makes me stronger...*Friedrich Nietzsche*

*

Love is the most beautiful thing to have, hardest thing to earn and the most painful thing to lose...*Unknown*

This book is dedicated to my precious children;
Ethan, Prada and Antonio

~1~

Mary always had a fear of flying so when she heard the engine on the plane stutter she immediately gripped the hand of her beloved husband Victor. Mary was travelling to Chicago for the third time that month. Her work schedule had her travelling to different cities throughout the year. Mary is the owner of a lucrative and well established brokerage firm with a vast clientele and a growing demand for her real estate services. She built the firm from the ground up, a task she was proud of but never bragged about. It could have been that Mary was very pleasing to the eye of most men but rumour had it she owned the best Brokerage firm around town. It was never her shining beauty that allowed her success to flourish, although it helped. Ultimately her business was a success because she was good at what she did.

Mary became very well known in New York. With her face plastered all over billboards, transit and buildings throughout the inner city, it was hard not to notice her. Mary's attempts at expanding her offices in Chicago proved to be harder than anticipated. The clients that have had the pleasure to meet with her in person witnessed her beauty, intelligence and charm firsthand. She didn't dance around any deals but rather cut to the chase and got the job done. Most men were naturally attracted to her looks first, with her business skills coming secondary but Mary always kept her business professional. Her luscious and voluminous black hair accented by her equally beautiful blue eyes was known to draw in her male clientele where as her talent and knowledge of her industry equally attracted female clients. Mary's long and lean legs were always a show stopper with the men especially when she wore her tailored skirt suits but it was her personality, intelligence and professional behaviour that her woman counterparts enjoy the most.

"Hey, not too tight," Victor jokingly said as Mary squeezed his hand tight. Victor was the only one who truly knew Mary inside and out. Next year, they were celebrating their tenth wedding anniversary. Victor already had the celebration planned and set in motion. Mary loved Victor's innate ability to keep everything organized and strategically planned without the slightest onset of stress. She joked about his low stress level being the only reason she married him. Victor knew better. He was the epitome of good looking and charming. Victor easily had a choice of women at any given time of the day. Standing at six feet tall, olive complexion and gleaming white teeth, Victor was pretty confident with himself. Women loved his full head of dark wavy hair and his fat wallet. He was overly generous with his money and most women socializing in his group knew that. When it came time to settle down and start a family, choosing a wife was a no-brainer for him. A woman like Mary was always on his radar so when he first met her, he knew just how to captivate her heart.

"I hate flying," Mary muttered.

"I wasn't aware of that," Victor lied. Clearly Victor thought it was best to use humour to keep the aircraft turbulence off the mind of his beloved. It wasn't unusual for Mary's mood to go from good to bad in a flash, especially if she felt threatened. Keeping with the teasing moment Victor decided to joke about the flight attendant checking him out.

"Oh please, get a grip," Mary said. "She's not checking you out, she's merely doing her job and making sure this plane isn't crashing." She leaned her head back on the plush leather backrest. Mary closed her eyes and pretended the turbulence was of no bother to her. She allowed her thoughts to take her to a darker time in her life. Although her past memories were not kind or meaningful, she tried to convince herself that the constant remembrance would help her emotionally heal. A time long ago before she even knew Victor, Mary's life was something you would only witness in a movie, or rather a horror story. Long before Mary learned the art of being strong willed and how to keep a stone faced facade, she was a delicate flower easily influenced in search for a promise of a happily ever after. She could feel her heart crushing all over again every time she allowed herself to think about him. She thought for sure he was her happily ever after.

Mary let go of Victor's hand abruptly and told him she was tired and wanted to rest. Victor obliged knowing all too well that Mary was allowing herself to be violated by her own inner demons and there was nothing he could do about it. Although they talked about it on a few select occasions, Mary never sought professional help after her breakup with Richard.

It still seemed inconceivable to Mary. How could she have been so blind? How could she have not known? How could she fool herself into thinking they were meant to be together, perfect for one another. How could it be that Mary hadn't noticed Richard had slipped away from her? How very manipulating and abusive he had become. How did it all change so suddenly? Why did she allow herself to be manipulated in such a horrible way? Was it already moving in that direction but she just chose not to notice? Everything seemed to be as it should be...until...until it wasn't...until Anna. The not knowing part made Mary feel like such an idiot, so naive. She'd been so vulnerable flying to New York and Chicago making real estate deals while Richard was making partners in his law firm. Perhaps they were both too busy to keep their relationship solid. Everyone who knew them thought they had a concrete relationship. It was a perfect blend of love, admiration and respect for one another and everyone witnessed it whenever they were together. When they were alone, that's when Mary had to become the person she desperately didn't want to be. She had to climb deep within herself, close the world out and put on her best performance as if her life depended on it, and sometimes it did.

Mary could hear the flight attended asking Victor if he wished to have another drink but Mary chose to ignore both the attendant and Victor's response. All she wanted to do is think back to the days she spent with Richard and try to make sense of it all. Part of her thought that if she figured out all the ways the relationship went wrong, she could ensure never to repeat those mistakes again. If only Anna hadn't come along and destroyed everything that seemed normal in her life then maybe things would have be different. Mary often placed the blame of their soured relationship on herself. If she wasn't so self consumed in building her career and business then maybe she would have seen all the warning signs. Maybe if Mary blamed herself she could try to make sense of it all, possibly figuring out why men seemed to turn to an Anna of sorts.

~2~

Richard was like no other man she had ever been with. His appearance was youthful as were his mannerisms but his wisdom matched his 49 years of life. Richard always dressed in fine tailored suits that made his shiny black hair seem that much more suave. His sharp cheekbones and chiselled jaw line made him look the part of clever attorney. Mary was twenty five years his junior. She had herself convinced her youth was what attracted Richard to her. He enjoyed being popular with young ladies. Richard appeared to relish in the flock of soaring hormones that surrounded his every move but there was something special in Mary that stopped Richard's gigolo ways. They worked very well together and Mary knew she could rely on him to keep her New York real estate deals clean and free of lawsuits. Being new in the business, Mary wanted to ensure she was building a reputable business with repeat clientele. New York deals rendered lucrative commissions and Mary quickly made a name and a large fortune for herself in the market. She was fairly confident

Richard had a big part in her success but he would never take the credit from her.

She quickly fell in love with Richard and his charm. She often flew to New York to spend the weekend with him. Soon enough, Mary found herself in New York more than her own apartment in Toronto. It was only natural for Richard to ask her to move in with him. He lived in a beautiful and spacious apartment in the upper east side of New York. She quickly adapted to the beautiful but very expensive neighbourhood. Richard and Mary would spend most of their weekends dining at one of the local eateries and afterwards strolling through the streets holding hands and frolicking at every crosswalk. It was an exceptional relationship and they spent most of their free time together. While they both travelled a great deal for work, they managed to keep an intense bond with one another. Mary had no real complaints about Richard and as far as she knew Richard had none of her. They argued periodically over menial things but that was mainly due to their strict and busy schedules. Sometimes Richard would need to be away for an entire weekend and Mary was mostly disappointed that they would have to cancel their plans. For the most part, Richard and Mary were the perfect power couple rising to the top of New York's corporate ladder. Richard spoke of marriage on a number of occasions with Mary which always excited her but he never offered her a promise or an engagement ring. She never showed concerned with the small details of their relationship. In her mind she was convinced he would pop the question at just the right moment in time. Mary was never alarmed with the fine print of their relationship and perhaps her inexperience allowed Richard the upper hand in their relationship. Mary was very giving of herself to him, mentally and physically. When Richard returned from his weekend travels, Mary was always ready and willing to keep him satisfied. Richard would often find Mary dressed in some scantily clad outfit holding a glass of their best Merlot for him to sip on and unwind. She often had a romantic mood set with light music lingering in the background and scented candles flickering in the aroma filled den. The light of the fireplace would cast a sexy shadow giving the grand piano a mysterious shape that seemed to hide in the corner of the dimly lit room. Richard enjoyed Mary's effort she put into their relationship. No matter how tired he was from his business trips he always managed to make passionate love to her. He was good at making sure Mary knew he still found her very attractive. Over the years their love making became more intense and seemingly more aggressive. Richard was Mary's first sexual relationship and she enjoyed learning from him. She never thought to question why their acts of love making became so physically intense. She figured it was a natural progression in all relationships. Mary wanted to keep their sex life fresh and untarnished. She was always willing to please Richard until one day their love making turned toxic. Richard started asking Mary to perform unusual and degrading sexual acts. Although Mary constantly pleased Richard with random acts of sex to his liking, Richard took to challenging her with aggressive name calling and forceful penetration. Mary was aware that she had to speak to Richard about their relationship, but she feared his reaction. Although she was embarrassed to talk about their private encounters, Mary knew she needed to place boundaries on their intimacy. That evening Richard came home in an unusually foul mood. Mary thought it was best to offer him a glass of wine as she regularly did. She hoped the wine would relax him after his long day at work. All day she prepared and coached herself on how she was going to confront him about his sexual mannerisms. It was a very difficult conversation to bring up but Mary found the courage to ask him about it anyway. Richard's response was not what Mary expected it to be. Their conversation that night revealed the unthinkable but it also gave Mary the out she subconsciously prayed for.

~3~

Mary adjusted her head and put her armrest in an upward position for a more comfortable placement in her seat on the aircraft. Thinking back to the *Richard* days, as Mary often referred that part of her life as; made her fidget and become uncomfortable in her own skin. Richard's affair with Anna had been culminating for nearly half a year. That much he told her. Richard loved Mary but the temptation of beautiful women and a growing desire for wild sex seemed to overrule his logical thinking and commitment to one woman. His sexual fantasies were becoming too hard to feed and he so much as told Mary that he respected her too much to ask her to fulfill his inner desires and passion for his unusual and aggressive sex demands. Mary would not agree to anal penetration or being mildly strangled while he called her names like bitch, slut and whore. Richard had turned into a monster, an aggressor of sorts. He started to live this secret life that Mary could not and would not be part of. She started to dislike herself for allowing Richard to please himself on a regular basis with whatever means he felt fit. Sometimes Mary would agree to disturbing acts in hopes that he would quit fooling around with other women. Most of the time, Richard would climax quickly and they would carry on with their everyday activities like two civilized citizens. When Richard was not in a sexual rage, he was the most adoring and attentive partner to her. He often brought her gifts of jewellery and perfumes from the top designers. He would promise her more time together and spoiled her with trips to exotic islands. She often thought of calling off their relationship but could never bring herself to do it. Mary felt trapped. She became recluse and concentrated on her work more and more. Oddly enough, the more she allowed herself to be victimized, the more successful she became in her career. Although Richard was abusive to her in the privacy of their home, he treated her like a queen in the general public. He adored her honour and commitment to his needs and valued her gorgeous body. They would often go to the gym together and he would whisper that he was going to give it to her hard in the sauna afterwards. Mary would flash him a smile but she knew she was slowly losing herself internally. Every vile action he forced upon her, Mary felt a piece of her inner strength and structure chip away. Piece by piece, her hollowing soul made room for her body to crumble. Mary hated when he used vulgar words toward her. She knew the scenario all too well. After a torturous work out on her arms and abs, she would have to pretend she was enjoying Richard's cowardly attempts at love making. First he would slam her into the wall face first all while telling her to bend over so he could jam himself hard into her. Mary would scream out in pain which only aroused Richard more. He would then grab her hair and yank her head back while he vigorously forced his erect penis down her throat. He would say things like "suck it hard baby" and "get ready whore because my cock is ready to fuck you something good." As Richard's body quivered rampantly over her, Mary remained still and most importantly quiet. She knew by his uncontrollable shaking he was almost ready to finish his demon attack and the end of his vicious pleasure was nearing. Richard's finale was always the same. He would groan in pleasure and then tell Mary that he loved her. She was always happy to hear that she was loved and equally pleased to know he was fulfilled. Mary was petrified to find out what would happen if she could no longer keep him satisfied.

Mary was always ashamed and held her guilt and lack of innocence to herself. This was not the love making scenarios she envisioned enduring for the rest of her life, nor did she want it to become a familiar part of their everyday life. Love making was never that way in the romance novels she read growing up. Mary didn't have close friends or even family to talk to about her troubling relationship. She was raised by her widow aunt when her parents passed. Mary never knew the real reason of their deaths but the coroner confirmed death by natural gas inhalation. There was speculation as to how and why there was a gas leak in the house but some gossip columns rumoured it to be murder suicide. Mary always felt she was a burden to her aunt so she did what she thought was best and left her Aunt's house at the very tender and impressionable age of fourteen. Mary practically raised herself always cautious not to let anyone get too close to her. She never wanted to relive loosing someone she loved again. Her co-workers were the closest thing she had to friendships and clearly rough sex wasn't something you could casually bring up as dinner conversation with a colleague. Besides, she was Mary Templemead, a little naïve girl from Toronto who continued to work tirelessly in order to build her career, her empire. Mary

Templemead, the same naïve girl who wanted to prove her rise to stardom in New York City.

Mary always questioned herself why she didn't leave Richard sooner and why it took Anna to finally give her the courage she needed to get out. What was the hold Richard had over her? Why did she let it take control of her life? Surely Anna was enduring the same torture that flagged Mary's life for so many years. Years that can never be erased, redone or fixed. Mary would have to live with the mental scars and learn how to function as a victim in society that refused to end violence against women. Mary attempted to warn Anna about Richard but her attempts only portrayed her to be the jealous ex-girlfriend. She never went to the police either. Mary feared her perfectly polished career would be tarnished in the industry and she couldn't risk that. Not after all the years of hard work and devotion she poured into starting her career. She thought it would be best to continue on with her life and bury the physical torment. Mary also thought that time would heal her pain and careful self questioning would give her all the answers she would need to start healing. Victor advised her otherwise but Mary's stubbornness always silenced Victor's concerns. When Mary showed signs of emotionally breaking down, Victor would hold her gently and offer her soft words of comfort. He knew she would seek treatment in her own time. Over the past 9 years of their marriage, Victor had earned her trust, love and respect. It wasn't easy but Victor was always in it for the long run.

From the very first moment Victor laid eyes on Mary he sensed a frightened yet strong woman. They met while having a cappuccino at Café Reggio in New York. Victor's amiable mannerism and charming conduct caught the attention of Mary almost immediately. With a slight smirk that lit up his eyes and showed off his gleaming white teeth, Victor knew he could draw the attention of almost any woman he so desired. Mary was no exception to this rule. Her small frame instantly went limp as she realized his charming glance was aimed toward her. Victor seemed to glide across the Italian cafe and Mary knew his destination was fast approaching. She cleared her throat in anticipation of his quick arrival. She even glanced behind her quickly to see if there was anyone else sitting behind her that he may be approaching. Nope! Mary instantly felt nervous and very childlike. Was this hunk of a well dressed man coming to speak to her? What would she say to him? Mary felt terrified with every step he took, getting closer and closer to her. Without a word Victor sat down at her table. He was careful to position himself directly across from her. With his beautifully manicured fingernails, Victor stretched out his manly hand in an effort to introduce himself.

"How did I get so lucky to be in the right place at the right time?" he blurted out taking her hand into his.

"Excuse me?" Mary answered desperate not to shine a spotlight on her nervous and trembling self.

"Much like the atmosphere in this establishment, I find you to be intoxicating. I am drawn to you and find it difficult to look away. It's like the universe has purposely drawn us together on this unusually warm winter day in order for us to meet one another. I can't help myself, I just had to come over and meet you," Victor declared.

"That's very charming," Mary said blushing and still holding the handsome man's hand.

"I am in the presence of pure beauty, and I just wanted to let you know before we parted ways. I am hoping we will meet again but something tells me your heart belongs to another man," Victor intuitively stated.

Still holding hands, Mary informed him of her recent break like a scared child making confession for the first time.

"You're shaking, are you okay?" Victor asked with tender sincerity.

Mary quickly retracted her petit hand. She wasn't aware that she was trembling. Embarrassed, she announced her departure.

"I need to go, there's somewhere I have to be," she lied.

"I'm sorry," Victor quickly said. "Please don't go! I didn't mean to offend you. I wasn't trying to pry into your business, I just wanted..."

Mary quickly stood up and was in the midst of excusing herself when Victor arose from the table as well. His tall physique made Mary weak at the knees. How could Mary even think this man was attractive so quickly after her break up from Richard? Victor's manly visage was outlined by freshly gown whiskers giving him that sexy facial shadow accenting his square jaw line that much more. The old Mary would have walked right out of that Café and into the streets of Greenwich Village never knowing who the handsome man was. That day was different. That day marked the day that changed Mary's life. It was the day that she decided to do something she had never done before. Mary took a step closer to Victor, delicately elevated her small frame up onto her tip toes and placed a passionate but simple kiss on the cheek of the handsome man's face. With that, Mary felt alive. She could feel her endorphins racing deep within her giving her that extra boost of courage to offer her phone number to the fine-looking stranger she just met.

~4~

Mary's in flight meal arrived. Mary loved flying first class, it always had it perks. Her pre ordered meal of the finest cut of steak and garlic mashed potatoes beautifully arranged on fine china was placed on her oversized tray. Mary's stomach immediately began to echo sounds of hunger but she was too deep into her own thoughts to notice. Mary robotically picked up her fork and carefully shuffled her way through the potatoes all while remembering how beautiful her first love with Richard started.

"Slow down Tiger," Victor said jerking Mary back to his world.

"I'm sorry, I didn't realize how hungry I was," Mary concluded.

"I'm glad you're eating. I know our schedules have been really hectic these days, and I hope you are taking care of yourself," Victor said with concern.

"I am," is all Mary could muster.

Mary always took pride in her health by going to the gym regularly and ensuring she was eating a well balanced diet rich in organic foods. Mary's always been a strong advocate of locally grown food, pure in its natural state and free from hormones and pesticides. She always reads her food labels ensuring the food she consumed was chemical free and not genetically modified. Victor adored her dedication to health and was thankful for her commitment to it. Her healthy habits that she flawlessly practiced on a regular basis helped Victor stay healthy too. After his car accident a few years back, Mary insisted Victor eat a well-balanced and organic whole diet in order for his body to heal. Fortunately, he did not sustain any lifelong injuries and was able to get back on his feet within a few short months. Victor doesn't speak of the accident very often but when he does, he always mentions how well Mary nursed him back to great health with her knowledge of super foods and healing agents.

"I don't doubt it for a moment," Victor added. "You've always known how to keep us healthy."

Only Victor does doubt it slightly this time. Telling Mary he had been observing her downward spiral in physical and mental health would only be spoken in poor judgment at this time. Victor's fully aware that Mary has been self punishing herself on an unconscious level. If she truly wanted to heal from her past, she would have to take responsibility for her actions and recognize her own chastisements. Seeking professional therapy would be her stepping stone to healing only she needed to come to that conclusion herself.

"Can I get the stewardess to fetch you something to drink?" Victor asked.

"Yes! Actually I would love a glass of Chardonnay please," Mary willingly answered. "This flight has me a little shaken up with all the turbulence. That put together with the horrible sleep I had last night has me in a bit of an uneasy state. Truthfully, I haven't been sleeping well for some time now."

"I have noticed you tossing and turning more than usual but I didn't bother saying anything to you. I presumed you're dealing with a big work load?" Victor said trying to sound innocent.

"Yes. That's it!" Mary regretfully lied. "You know me so well."

Victor sensed the hint of sarcasm in Mary's voice so he decided to leave well enough alone. Every time he tried to comfort or offer help to her these days, he experienced resistance. Aware of how independent Mary's been, he didn't want to intrude on her personal matter or space. She's always opened up to Victor on her own accord and this situation would serve to be no different. When Mary was ready to divulge her inner thoughts, feelings and fears, Victor would be the open and willing shoulder she needed.

"One glass of Chardonnay for my beautiful lady," Victor announced taking Mary by surprise.

Mary's constant escape in and out of the present moment slowly played on Victor's patience but he still said nothing. He wasn't even sure how he managed to keep his composure in check for this long. Mary's constant absence from their relationship was really driving a wedge between them.

"Oh, thank you," she coughed up. "I must have drifted somewhere else for a second."

"You've been doing that a lot lately. Can I help you out with your workload at all?" Victor offered.

"My work load?" Mary asked. "Oh! My workload," she reiterated as if she just understood the question for the first time.

Mary recognized that it wasn't her workload that was occupying her thoughts. In fact, it was her workload that allowed her to escape from her thoughts. If only she could work twenty four hours a day, she wouldn't have a moment to think of her past and how life scaring it has been.

The longer she allowed herself to continue to relive those horrible moments in time, the more she consented to her inner demons taking over her life.

"Something is clearly going on with you lately and I really want to be able to help you," Victor offered.

"You're sweet, really you are," Mary pledged.

"I'm not trying to be sweet," Victor clarified. His demeanor and tone turned very serious for the first time in their marriage.

"Well whatever you're trying to be, it doesn't go unnoticed," she informed him. "I've become aware of how much time and effort you've been putting into my well being these days and quite frankly it is getting a little annoying."

"Annoying? What on earth are you talking about?" Victor asked in a wounded whisper.

"You're constantly hovering and dotting on my every move and request! A glass of Chardonnay? Well yes, right away!" Mary mockingly said. "Car service…immediately! Another assistant…hired! Spa getaway…wouldn't have it any other way."

"You never mentioned any of this before," Victor spoke with concern. "If my love and attention to your needs are something of an annoyance to you, then why would you not tell me?"

"Victor! I can't tell you anything anymore. Every time I mention anything to you, you manage to take the situation over and offer a resolution without even consulting me on the final decision. I am a woman who needs no man to help me in life. I have been through too much and I have witnessed enough to wear the proud woman badge on my shoulders loud and swollen with pride!"

"Okay. I'm getting the sense that this isn't about me anymore," Victor questioned.

"About you! Why does it always have to be about you?" Mary asked, getting more annoyed with every comment.

"It doesn't have to be about me. I'm simply asking a rhetorical question that clearly you are taking too personal," he proclaimed. "Why do you have this innate ability to turn everything around on me? I'm not the one with a problem. I'm not the one who is never present in our conversations anymore. I'm not the one who is burying themselves in their work so they don't have to deal with the real problem."

"Who the hell do you think you are?" Mary said defiantly.

Mary never raised her voice to Victor in their entire relationship. Mary was generally soft spoken for the most part unless she needed to show authority within her work environment. Her attitude and compassion for her husband had always been nothing short of love, respect and admiration.

"I think I'm your husband," Victor answered. "I'm pretty sure that as a husband, I've done nothing but offer reverence and solace to you and your needs. I never expected you to speak to me with such anger and despotism."

"Is that what you think? Despotism? Why can't we just have a civil argument without a cut throat accusation?" Mary stated.

"I've never seen this side of you before. I'm really not sure what I have done to deserve this type of treatment from you but I assure you I will and I can leave you to your own demise," he blurted out immediately wishing he could retract the statement.

"Are you threatening me?" Mary asked.

"I'm not threatening you Mary. I'm merely stating a fact," he announced.

"A fact! Well that fact sounds an awful lot like an intimidation tactic," she added.

"Mary, you know I love you and I think this discussion is going nowhere. My concern for you and your mood toward everything lately is purely innocent. I'm not implying anything or trying to egg you on in any manner. I love you! I'm concerned about you. I see you drifting off and I just want to ensure you are okay," he affirmed.

Mary relaxed her tense shoulders and offered him a genuine smile.

"Thank you," she whispered as her eyes start to fill with tears.

"Oh baby, please don't cry," Victor pleaded. "You are my world. I've known this from the very moment I saw you. You are everything to me and there is nothing in this world I wouldn't do for you."

"I love you too, and please trust that there is nothing you need to be concerned with. I am fine. Sometimes I just get wrapped up in my own thoughts," Mary tried her best to explain.

"Okay then its settled. I won't pry or ask anymore," he said.

"It's not that I don't want to share with you, it's just that there is nothing to share," Mary declared as if trying to convince him and perhaps she was trying to convince herself as well.

They both reclined their seats back and clinked their glasses together. The toast was a sort of affirmation to one another.

"Here's to our first official fight," Mary claimed.

With a snicker and a giggle they both retracted to their prospective drinks and personal thoughts. Mary was sure Victor was psychoanalyzing every word they spoke. Victor was sure Mary had gone back to her well kept secret thoughts.

~5~

Mary had always dreamed of making a life with Richard but somehow was still surprised when he asked her to take the next big step with him.

"I don't know what to say to you Richard," Mary spoke calmly.

"Just say yes! Yes that you will move in with me. Yes that you will accept New York as your new city of residence and yes that you will commit to me fully," he answered.

"I would like to give it some thought," Mary softly said as she leaned over to deliver him a soft kiss. "There is just so much to think of. I would have to learn how to navigate around the city, move my office to somewhere appealing to both my commute and my existing clientele and..."

"There is no need to stress about it baby. I will give you all the time you need to think this through but allow me the privilege to take care of all the details of your move and you won't need to even lift a finger. We are a team now. You, me and our beautiful apartment in which you can decorate to your liking I might add," he proclaimed hoping his offer was enticing enough for her to agree.

Mary's inner gut was throwing out powerful messages of disapproval with a constant pain. Her heart on the other hand was beating out the perfect fairytale rendition of a glamorous and successful powerhouse Broker. Her head told her to be practical and to offer some serious thought to such a big life changing step.

"I don't need to think about it. I'm in! Let's do this together, I'm ready," she blurted out clearly following her heart and ignoring all the other warning signs her brain and gut spat out.

"Then it's settled. I will make the arrangements for everything in the morning. Don't you worry your pretty self with any details of moving. I will have my assistant at your beck and call any time of day should you need her and please Mary, use the resources I'm offering," Richard scolded.

And with that statement Richard turned on his heal, completely satisfied with the acceptance of his proposal. True to his word, Richard had placed a call to his assistant Anna immediately. Mary could hear his voice resonating through the corridor leading to the bedroom. His strong and very masculine tone always made Mary's heart skip a beat. She could hear Richard giving Anna orders to call for the moving company and to ensure the transition went as smoothly as possible. Richard also made sure to have the extra bedroom set up as a home office so that Mary could comfortably conduct business immediately while scouting for suitable office space.

In the ensuing months, Richard ricocheted between adorning love and verbal torment. Mary found it increasingly hard to concentrate on her work. She was constantly analysing her everyday actions in order to keep Richard from spinning out of control. It was the beginning of her slow road to loneliness that would ultimately haunt her every waking moment only she didn't know it yet. Mary would often become recluse in the comfort of her own home. Now that she shared her personal living space with Richard, she felt that she was under constant surveillance. Richard had this innate ability to know what Mary's daily activities consisted of and even what and who she spoke to. She always chalked it up to coincidence but with Richard's new character change, Mary started paying more attention to her so called privacy. When speaking on her cell phone, she often hovered into a corner cupping her mouth; trying to quiet her already whispered voice. Mary was vigilant not to leave any business contracts or proposals carelessly placed around the apartment. Never wanting to breach any of her client's confidentiality, she often hid her briefcase in different locations within the apartment. She couldn't figure out why or how there appeared to be so many specific topic correlations that Richard would sporadically bring up in conversation. Mary started to feel that their relationship was slowly withering away into empty meaning and that made her sad. Originally they had been two strong independent people working vigorously to establish themselves into a chosen career but somehow over time, Mary felt like she had lost a part of herself to Richard. His dominating antics were breaking her down. Whenever Richard would ask to set a date for marriage, Mary would feel like all the air was being squeezed out of her lungs. The warning signs of her toxic relationship were literally crushing her, but Mary chose to chalk the air deprivation up to wedding anxiety and a little bit of cold feet. For what she researched about planning a wedding, these were all normal feelings and most brides; if not all of them, go through these awkward and unwanted feelings.

As their one year anniversary of living together was nearing, Mary thought a romantic dinner with soft music and wine would be a perfect way to celebrate. They both had been working endless days and nights building their careers. As much as Mary felt she had changed over the past year, so were the many faces Richard wore so openly now. Mary took great pride in her appearance. Their anniversary night was no exception. She strategically placed her sexy lingerie on the bathroom shelving unit hidden under some towels that way she could secretly change into them after dinner. She was sure to apply just a little more makeup to her face, just the way Richard liked it, to ensure satisfaction for her man. Mary mentally prepared for her submissive role. A role she would need to play for Richard in hopes he would be satisfied with her. Her evening attire was carefully picked out as well. She chose a pastel blue Chanel skirt suit in which she had altered so that the skirt would fall exactly one inch above her knee; paired with a strappy stiletto that oozed sexy with a hint of bad ass. Richard loved when Mary would show her long adoring legs but would often fly off the handle if too much leg was exposed. He always told her that she should act like a whore with him in private but look like a lady in public. He had her convinced that all men view women as tempting bitches because they dressed like sluts. Mary never wanted to be viewed like that by anyone let alone another man. She always felt like men undressed her with their eyes regardless of what she was wearing. Richard was sure to prove that his theory was correct by pointing out any and all men that looked her way.

Knowing Richard was due home anytime, Mary lit all the candles that she placed around dining room. She put the Champagne on ice and set her music playlist on shuffle. Mary chose a soft blend of classic rock and acoustic blues for background noise. She double checked her makeup and hair in the oversized mirror that hung in the entrance of their studious apartment. She caught herself checking and double checking all her dinner arrangements while waiting for the arrival of her beloved Richard.

"He's only twenty minutes late," she said to herself out loud.

Mary knew all too well the hectic schedule Richard endured with his practice. Now that he had made partners within the firm, Richard constantly put in extra long hours to ensure his workload didn't get out of hand. She was well aware that his long office hours and constant work pressure exasperated his declining mood, but she thought a romantic evening could take his mind off it all. Thinking back, Mary recognized that Richard appeared to be in a constant bad mood but it was all a façade.

"This is exactly why I need to cheer him up today and show him how much he is loved and adored," she stated to her mirrored reflection adoring her new shade of red lipstick.

Mary opened the chilled Champagne and poured herself a glass. She surprisingly gulped the entire flute down. Mary quickly refreshed her glass and stammered over to the mirror encouraging a conversation with the girl staring back at her. Mary gazed at her reflection with a blank look as she witnessed her very own eyes welling up with tears. Peering down at her wristwatch, she openly declared that Richard was now an hour late. Mary sheepishly glided over to the Champagne and took a swig directly from the bottle. She laughed out loud picturing Richard's disapproving expression and feeling pleased with herself for her devious behaviour. Placing the bottle back on the dining table, Mary removed her dress jacket and unbuttoned her dress shirt slightly in order to allow air to circulate around her neck. She wasn't sure if it was the Champagne fueling her heat or if it was Richard's tardiness. Mary pulled out a dining chair to sit on and carefully leaned down to unbuckle her strappy shoes. She felt defeated as her blouse loosely hung open while her hair dangled in front of her face. Between her soft blubbering tears and the soft rock playing, Mary didn't hear

Richard enter the apartment. As Mary looked up, Richard was already advancing toward her. She quickly rose to her feet and attempted to straighten her hair back into place. Her cheeks were lustrous, adoring the perfect rose hue from her crying. Her hair was faultlessly messed as if purposely styled to look that way. Mary's open blouse was revealing enough to show her lace bra and her puckered lips resembling a pout was enough to excite Richard.

"You look gorgeous," Richard proclaimed.

With a slight grin Mary stammered, "I was crying but thank you for the compliment."

Richard advanced closer to her and extended his arms in a gentle manner. Mary really needed Richard to hold her and tell her that everything would be okay; that he was sorry for being late. Instead, Richard tugged her closer and ripped open her shirt revealing her breast fully. He pulled up her bra without any regard to her current state of mind and began sucking on her breasts. She was immediately turned on by his touch even though she wanted to push him away and express how deeply angry she felt by his constant lack of consideration and respect for her as a woman. He cupped her soft breast, engulfing her entire erect nipple in his wet mouth. He was sure to circulate his tongue around her nipple while biting down. Mary could feel his immediate arousal pressed up against her body. Her heart was pounding as she was sure Richard could feel the beats of her heart resonating through his teeth. Mary wanted him to stop but every time she tried to pull away he gripped her harder. In the heat of the moment, Richard grabbed Mary's hair and tugged her head back. He advanced his wet lips to her bare neck and proceeded to lift her skirt for easy access. Mary started to tense up knowing all too well that his attempt at love making was turning aggressive. When he felt her resisting he pushed her onto the couch and forcefully separated her legs so that he could devour her womanhood. Mary closed her eyes knowing she couldn't win the battle. Richard tore her matching lace underpants off and thrust himself into her. The weight of his body was crushing her which only added to her panic. Her attempt to reposition his weight only proved to be more arousing to Richard. The more Mary squirmed the more she inadvertently stimulated him. At the height of his climax he moaned, "That was great Anna."

"Who's Anna?" Mary clamoured.

"What are you talking about Mary?" Richard responded.

"Anna! You said that was great Anna!" she bellowed.

"I think you're mistaken darling. I didn't say Anna, I said again," he quickly retorted.

"Alright," Mary agreed. With those lingering thoughts, she quickly rose to her feet and proceeded to collect her torn garments. She was careful not to bend in front of Richard because she didn't want to give him any ideas of a do over to make up for his possible name slip up. As she gathered her belongings Richard told her how much he loved her and that she was a good lay. His constant belittling and crude statement toward her were really wearing thin. Mary's self worth was slowly crumbling.

"Ummm," Mary started by clearing her throat. Her hesitant start only proved her nervousness. "I know we are pretty comfortable living together and it is our one year anniversary but I'm feeling a little intimidated by your language and aggressive love making," she finished, finally getting the nerve to address his unwelcomed behaviour.

"What do you mean? I've always told you how much I find you attractive and how I love fucking you," Richard stated.

"That's exactly it. Your choice of words can sometimes make me feel like less than a woman and truthfully I find it offensive," Mary informed him softly.

"Mary, I'm sorry you feel that way. I like talking dirty to you. You shouldn't take it so seriously. I think that you can be over sensitive sometimes. There's nothing wrong with me telling you how much you turn me on. You get me so horny and when I come home to see you half naked with your shirt undone and your lips all puckered up and moist it makes me so hard. I'm getting hard now thinking about you. Come on, give me a blowjob," Richard rousingly said as he groped himself to entice his growing erection.

"Seriously Richard, this is what I'm talking about!" Mary continued. "You don't take me serious anymore. I'm not just your play toy who sexually satisfies you at your every demand."

"You're not?" Richard jokingly said. "Please Mary! I could have any woman I want and I chose you. We're engaged to be married. I'm just having a little fun. Lighten up a little would you?"

"Richard, I know you like joking around but there are times when you can make me feel cheap and worthless. Just the other day you pointed to a random guy and told me he was checking me out. I believe your exact words were *I bet he's picturing your tits cupped in his hands right now,"* Mary said sheepishly.

"He was!" Richard hollered.

"Then you attempt to mark your territory by putting your arm around my waist and pull me into your jealous clutch," Mary said.

"My jealous clutch?" Richard laughed. "Like this?" Richard pulled her naked body on top of his, quickly flipping her over and holding her down on the ground.

"You're hurting me," Mary whimpered.

"You like it, so don't try to play innocent with me," he said in his own joking manner.

"You're getting very aggressive with your hugs," Mary added.

"I plan to show you aggressive over and over again," Richard assured her. He pushed himself into her again forcing her to scream in pain. "This is the way we should be fucking all the time," Richard moaned as he anally penetrated her.

"No, please stop," Mary cried out.

"Your ass is so warm and tight, it makes your pussy feel really loose. This is the proper way to please a real man," he demanded.

"Owe, please stop," she pleaded.

"Not a chance baby, I'm gonna cum," he finished.

Mary's tears were visible on her face when Richard pulled her head to the side to kiss her. She wondered how someone who claimed to love her so much could violate her that way. Better yet, why did she allow it to happen? Mary quickly got into the shower, disgusted with his actions. She was desperate to wash away the sin and violation she endured.

~6~

Victor was always watchful of Mary's actions. Her most recent emotional breakdown was the hardest one he had witnessed. Waiting on stand-by for her emotional crash was not an option anymore. He knew he had to take action.

"Are you okay Mary? Mary! Mary!" Victor was frantic.

Mary opened her eyes, visibly shaken. Tears flooded her cheeks while she openly wept. Mary quickly tried to pull herself together so Victor wouldn't start hounding her. She's always been very protective about her past and the torment she suffered. Reliving the nightmare with another person was too excruciating for her to imagine. Although Victor was aware of the details of her past, he was equally cautious and sensitive about her feelings. He knew bringing up the past was painful for her which often triggered nightmares.

"I'm fine!" Mary barked.

Victor always respected Mary's privacy on this particular matter but he knew it was time to step in and make sure Mary sought appropriate council for her inner haunting.

"Mary, I know I've said this in the past to you but I really think it's time to seek therapy of some sorts. I will attend with you if you feel more comfortable but I really think that you are in need of help," he tried to say in the most comforting voice he could. "You constantly shut me down and all I'm trying to do is help you. Let me help you," he pleaded.

"I thought I had all my feelings sorted out. I'm not sure I can open up to anyone for judgement. I should have stopped it when it was happening. I'm scared," Mary told him.

"I know you're scared Mary but honestly honey, I can't take it anymore. I'm watching you fall apart in front of my eyes and I feel sick to my stomach when it's happening. You may not know this but your constant push back and lack of self worth is killing me. I can't idly stand by and watch it anymore. I'm trying desperately to help you and I've asked you to seek help on a number of occasions but seriously, if you don't help yourself get past this inner torment..." The remaining part of the sentence was too difficult for Victor to say out loud. He paused for a brief moment but he knew the words needed to be said. "You give me no choice but to leave you," Victor told her.

Wiping away her tears and visibly shaken by his threats to end their marriage, Mary agreed to seek help but on her terms only. She would research the therapy types and choose accordingly. She also assured Victor that she would be able to handle the process on her own.

"I appreciate your willingness to accompany me but I'm certain I can do this on my own. I will do this on my own. I can do this on my own," Mary said.

As the plane prepared for descend, Mary enthusiastically started researching therapists on her laptop. It was her feeble attempt to show Victor she was serious about therapy. She felt a sense of calm overcome her. She looked over at Victor and offered a smile, mainly to show her strength but more importantly her willingness to listen to him; and save their marriage. Mary knew she was broken inside and it made her sad, even on her most happy days.

They walked through the airport hand in hand, not saying a word to each other mostly in fear of sparking a new argument. Victor was desperate to try and help Mary and the only way he knew how was to console her. His attempts to be supportive only resulted in Mary pushing him further away. He could see that she was internalizing her emotions and that scared him the most. He had observed her sleep patterns change and her increased anxiety. Victor knew her mood change stemmed from her unresolved past conflicts, but Mary was adamant on blocking all communication about it with Victor. She continually insisted that she was fine but Victor knew better.

The past few weeks had been the hardest for Victor. He could only approach Mary so many times about seeking help before she went into complete emotional shutdown. It was pouring rain the morning he told her he couldn't take it anymore for the second time in their marriage. They were both rushing from a late morning rise when their conversation quickly escalated into a fight. Unable to settle the disagreement before they both rushed out the door to their prospective meetings was the perfect recipe for a disastrous day. Victor couldn't shake his uneasy feeling knowing Mary was so fueled with anger and depression when he left her in the morning. As the afternoon drizzle faded so did Victor's guilt for pushing Mary to seek help. The more he thought about it, the more he realized that he would have to give her an ultimatum. No more oscillating between happy and sad moods anymore. The first time he threatened to leave her seemed to give Mary the push she needed to start researching therapists but not enough to book the appointment. Victor wanted more out of his marriage and he was sure Mary did as well. There would be nothing left to say now except how sorry he was that she has to go through this. He envisioned different scenarios but chose to focus on the only one he thought would help. He thought about quitting his firm to focus solely on Mary and her recovery but deep down he knew that wouldn't help her. Although the idea was appealing, the thought quickly fizzled. Victor leaned up against his office wall peering out the window watching the traffic below move slowly along the busy streets. The more he thought about leaving Mary the more he got choked up. Without even realizing it, tears were streaming down his unshaven face. He desperately wanted to run to her office, throw his arms around her tightly and never let her go. Instead, he would work a full day and meet up with her later in the privacy of their home they shared and break the news to her. Victor never thought the day would come when he would have to speak those words. Looking down at his wedding ring, Victor placed his index finger and his thumb around the circular band and contemplated removing it. While debating the idea in his head, he twirled the band around and around his finger remembering the day he said his vows. *For rich or for poor, in sickness and in health, in good times and in bad times until death do us part*. Those were the words he remembered. He honestly believed those words at the time, but now he could see no other resolution. He pulled his wedding ring off and carefully placed it in his pocket for safe keeping. Not wearing his wedding ring would ensure he would follow through with his ultimatum, or at least the opportunity to open to the conversation. There would be no more going back on his decision. The pain and anguish of witnessing Mary torment herself with past fears and personal tortures was killing him. Victor started to tear up again. He knew that he was the one that needed to stay strong in order to save their marriage. He was also aware that sometimes letting go could be the start of the healing process. After careful consideration, Victor placed his wedding ring back on his finger, exactly where he was comfortable having it. After all, he still loved Mary with all of his heart. He convinced himself he was not leaving Mary but rather he would push her in the right direction to seek help. Tonight, he would have to approach her tenderly and try his best to explain why he was leaving her. Victor chose his words wisely in hopes that his practiced statements would guide her to the treatment she so desperately needed. Without hesitation, Victor grabbed his suit jacket from the back of his chair and headed out to the hallway to wait for the elevator. Without saying a word to anyone in his office, Victor went straight home to face the hardest night of his life. He reached his final destination in a timely manner only he was not so eager to get home that day. Victor usually pranced through the door anxiously anticipating his good evening kiss with the love of his life. That night was drastically different. An uneasy feeling quickly crept up inside him as he casually walked through the door to his once happy home. He could clearly see Mary in the kitchen preparing a meal for them to eat. He stood still and in silence observing her seemingly effortless movements. Her silhouette gliding across the kitchen with such poise and elegance, he almost forgot his reason for coming home so early.

"I need to go back to Toronto for awhile," Mary told Victor without turning around. "I know it is bad timing but my career is on the line and I have to mediate an important real estate deal that can't go wrong. I'm the only one who can make sure this deal goes through."

"How long is awhile?" Victor asked with concern as he entered the loft apartment.

"A few weeks, maybe a month? As long as it takes for me to make sure this deal finalizes," Mary replied.

"Is this really necessary Mary? I mean, I really need to talk to you about a few pressing matters that need immediate attention. I will make arrangements with my office so I can go with you that way I can be close by if you need me," he offers.

"Thank you but no. I need to take care of business like a big girl and I promise that I will keep in constant contact with you while I'm there. I think it's exactly what I need right now and it couldn't come at a better time," Mary proudly said.

Mary had been feeling the tension in her relationship for awhile. Victor's subtle hints about seeking therapy didn't go unnoticed to Mary. Although she and Victor always prided on their open communication skills, Mary knew she had to keep her mixed emotions to herself for now. If she divulged her inner torment to Victor, she knew he would try to talk her into immediate counselling. She just wasn't ready for him to be actively involved. She promised herself that she would seek help while away on business that way Victor would be none the wiser. Mary was adamant to come back to Victor a new woman.

An emotionally strong new woman, just like she always envisioned herself to be. There would be no room for error. No need to worry or fuss on her behalf. She was sure she had everything under control. All her emotions in check, only she knew she was kidding herself. She was in need of some help, some serious help.

"Dinner smells amazing," Victor said to break the silence.

"Thank you. It's your favourite tonight. Stuffed pasta shells filled with a blend of cheese, sausage and spinach," Mary responded. Making Victor's favourite dish was Mary's pathetic attempt to keep her husband happy. She knew only too well that she was receiving a failing grade in every other area of their marriage at this point in her life. Her past memories were holding her hostage. Over the years, her history slowly oozed its way into her everyday life like a slow toxic spill. Her agony, pain and misery of long ago didn't disappear when she finally gained the courage to leave the monster she once loved. Instead, the pain remained locked inside her trickling into her ever moment of life and poisoning any chance of pure happiness. Mary knew she had to seek therapy in order to keep her marriage to Victor.

As the evening progressed, Mary and Victor found very little to speak about. They were both lost in their own thoughts. A few times Victor would open his mouth in an attempt to speak but would stop himself just before the whisper of his breath left his mouth. He couldn't fathom speaking the words of leaving her at this moment. Not after Mary just announced she would be leaving their home for a month. Maybe this temporary separation would be the answer Victor was desperately seeking. Without witnessing Mary's constant emotional breakdowns, Victor would be able to concentrate on the proper steps to ensure her healing. He knew at that moment that he would have to get in touch with his old school buddy who lived in Toronto. Victor would make sure that if he couldn't physically be there to protect Mary then he would have to have someone else do it for him.

~7~

Mary placed her bags down beside her with a sigh. Her arrival to Toronto didn't go without any hiccups. Without Victor by her side to keep her calm, Mary's flight dramatically exasperated her anxiety. Nonetheless, she conquered her first hurdle on her own which made her smile. After a quick glance around the airport, Mary picked up her bags, spotted her exit route and made her way to the outside world. Standing straight and tall, she attempted to hail a cab by extending her arm on a slight diagonal outward reach toward the street. Quickly, Mary realized she was not in New York anymore. Torontonians did not request modes of transportation the same way her New Yorker counterparts did. While shuffling through her Hermes bag for her cell phone, Mary wondered why her personal assistant didn't book her a taxi service of some sort. Mary felt a little out of sorts on the streets of Toronto while still impersonating her New York lifestyle. Realizing her upscale life in New York needed to be toned down a tad while staying in

Toronto, she quickly dialed a taxi service. Clutching onto her Louis Vuitton luggage while balancing her Hermes Birkin hand bag on her forearm, Mary internally wished her taxi would arrive sooner rather than later. She could feel the stares from strangers passing by. Mary placed her oversize sunglasses on to try and hide behind the stares and glares but that only seemed to attract more attention. She could hear the whispers and giggles of some young girls standing to her left convinced she was a movie star from some other part of the world visiting Toronto to film an upcoming box office hit. Mary quickly realized that the airline tags on her luggage gave away her whereabouts so she removed the tags and placed them in her pocket. Without being obvious, she turned so that her back was now facing the young girls. Mary wasn't ready to be in the background photo of their selfie picture. She could only imagine the tag line they would use while posting the picture on social media. When Mary noticed the taxi arrive curbside, she quickly jumped into the back seat letting the driver place her luggage into the trunk. She was never so happy to have tinted windows in her car service. Somehow or another, these young girls managed to create a scene which only prompted a larger crowd who then started to snap more pictures and gossip on who they speculated she was. It was that very moment Mary knew she needed to ditch the elite clothing and accessories and try to blend into her new home, even if it was only for a limited time.

"You've managed to attract quite a crowd," the cab driver stated.

"Believe me, it was not my intention," Mary explained.

"Are you some kind of movie star or something," he asked.

"Drive, just drive!" Mary blurted out noticing the crowd circling the taxi.

"Where to?" asked the taxi cab driver.

"Oh shit," Mary said. "Just start driving while I find my itinerary."

The cab driver did exactly what Mary asked and proceeded to take the cab from zero to sixty in no time flat. He instinctively headed towards the highway waiting for his proper destination to be told to him. Mary pulled out her itinerary and skimmed through the wording to find her hotel name booked by her assistant on her behalf.

"Four Seasons Hotel in Yorkville please," Mary blurted out.

"Very well Miss," he said without hesitation.

Mary's thoughts of her airport posse were easily distracted with her destination. There were a few select hotels that she stayed at when she traveled to Toronto. On one of her most recent trips to Toronto, Mary stayed at The Hazelton but preferred to stay at The Four Seasons. The Four Seasons was one of the hotels she always enjoyed staying at. Having access to all the fashionable shopping she desired as well as being able to relish in the best restaurants were some of her favourite perks the hotel's location had to offer. Even though her suite was equipped with a dining area and kitchen, Mary favoured evenings at local restaurants. Knowing that her taxi ride would last forty minutes, Mary took advantage of the time by placing a call to Victor. She wasn't sure why her hands where so shaky while dialing his personal cell number but she knew his calming voice would be all the reassurance she needed. When Victor answered her call, Mary's uneasy feeling seemed to vanish as quickly as it came on.

"Hi honey, how are you?" Victor immediately asked.

Unsure of how she felt about his question, Mary quickly answered with a simple and rather short response. "I'm fine."

"You know I'm just a phone call away should you need anything," Victor added.

"I know, I know! Without this sounding too callus, Victor could you please give me a little space? I have this big deal that I need to close and I want to make sure that all my thoughts and energy get poured into this deal. You know that the outcome of this transaction will affect my career so I want to make sure I am concentrating on nothing else but this," Mary stated.

"You called me." Victor was quick to point out. "I know how important your career is to you Mary, but I am your husband and I can't help but worry about you," Victor retorted.

"And you know that I have always been an independent woman who knows how to take care of myself," she claimed.

"You're right," Victor agreed. He knew all too well how stubborn and closed off Mary could be when she had something stuck in her head. Instead of bantering back and forth on the telephone with her, Victor decided to leave it alone. After all, his old school buddy Camden was going to make sure Mary was safe. Victor had already made the appropriate plans to ensure the love of his life was being watched and taken care of. Camden and Victor studied first year law together. After a challenging year,

Camden decided to change his career path and study psychology. Regardless of their career choices, Victor and Camden remained friends over the years. They had the type of friendship that needed no constant reminders of what a strong bond they shared back in law school. They could go months and sometimes years without speaking to one another and then pick back up where they left off. Social media was a great way to drop quick messages back and forth without taking any real time away from home or work life. With Victor being incredibly busy with his law practice, he could only imagine the tight schedule and long hours Camden kept with his patients. It had been a few years since Victor met up with Camden in person but nevertheless Camden was more than accommodating when Victor asked for the favour. Victor left it up to Camden on how he was going to approach Mary. He sent a text with an updated picture of what Mary looked like accompanied with her arrival time, date and where she would be staying while in Toronto. Camden responded with great fervour stating that's what friends were for, helping out when asked.

"I really do appreciate all that you do for me Victor, and knowing what an incredibly understanding husband you are helps too," Mary said convincingly.

"I love you Mary," Victor added.

"I love you too. I'll call you later when I'm all settled in," Mary finished.

As Victor ended the call, he smiled knowing the plan he had set in motion without Mary knowing was coming together nicely. He could successfully monitor her every move without her even knowing, thanks to Camden.

Mary looked out the car window caught up in deep thought about where her life had taken her. Her nervousness and anxiety only seemed to escalate knowing full well that she had lied to her husband about the supposed big deal she needed to close for her firm. In reality, Mary planed to settle into her new Toronto life before reaching out to her therapist. She would allow herself a week in Toronto before she attempted to schedule a therapy appointment. The week adjustment period seemed reasonable enough for her to collect her thoughts. Victor would be none the wiser of her deception.

"Have you been to Toronto before?" the driver asked.

Breaking Mary out of her deep thought she responded with a giggle, "Yes a few times."

"It's such a beautiful city," the driver added.

"Yes, a beautiful city it is! I'm looking forward to spending the next five weeks or so in this beautiful city," Mary declared.

"Five weeks! You will be staying at The Four Seasons Hotel for that long?" the driver inquired.

"That's the plan, but sometimes plans change. I've stayed at this Hotel a few times, one of my favourites to be honest. I enjoy the atmosphere and the relaxing spa after a hard day at work," Mary explained. "Only this time I'm not here for work."

"I'm going to give you my business card, and please call me directly should you need a ride around town anywhere. I will be sure to make myself available to you at any time of day," he announced making it clear so she understood his sincerity.

"That is very kind of you," Mary expressed. She took the business card from his tattooed hand looking over the printed details on it. Knowing she was not really in Toronto for business, Mary thought it would be a good idea to retain his business card and use him solely as a driver for whenever she needed to travel. After all, his business card did say personal driver and intelligence quotient. Although the business card title was rather vague and oddly titled Mary thought nothing more of it and placed the card in her purse. Having a personal driver would be a good start in trying to be inconspicuous within the city. Maybe it was a good idea that her assistant didn't book her a personal car service after all. Knowing how protective Victor was of her, Mary didn't put it past him to have the car service report back her every outing. Having found a personal driver on her own guaranteed her that Victor couldn't have them report back to him. Mary loved her husband but his over protective and sheltering behaviour traits were exactly what she was trying to escape.

"We are a short distance away from the hotel Mrs. You have my business card now, and please do not hesitate to call me for a ride anytime. Oddly enough, I reside close by so it will be no trouble at all," the driver explained.

Mary looked at the business card one last time before placing it back into her purse for safe keeping.

"Thank you Camden," Mary said. Unannounced to him, Mary planned on using his offered service to keep her husband from spying on her through a scheduled car service she was sure he'd hire.

"Camden! That is a unique name. Where have I heard that name before?" Mary asked out loud.

"It's really not that uncommon," Camden openly admitted while pulling up to the front entrance of The Four Seasons Hotel. "Call me anytime."

Mary handed over her credit card to pay for the taxi ride. She couldn't help but wonder how she recognized his name. She stared at his taxi licence clearly visible on his front visor. It read Camden Joseph date of issue February 25, 1999. Mary noticed that Camden had a few tattoos, but the words hate inscribed across his fingers on his left hand stood out the most. The letters looked to be etched in freehand, faded and uneven. Out of pure curiosity, Mary wanted to ask him about the tattoo but quickly decided against it. She was sure there was a bundle of buried pain behind the scarred letters. Much like her own pain etched deep within her soul, she was sure he wanted to leave the topic buried in his inner depth of silence.

"I know why your name sounds so familiar," Mary said with excitement.

Nervously Camden replied, "Umm, really? How?"

"My husband is friends with a Camden from years ago. He's an old law school friend," she told him.

"Oh! Nice," Camden said keeping it short.

"It was bugging me the whole ride here on how I recognized your name and now I finally figured it out," Mary stated.

"Fig…figured it out?" Camden said with a nervous stutter.

"Yes! I knew your name sounded familiar. Now I know why. It's not a popular name but low and behold I now know of two Camden's," Mary laughed.

Camden laughed along with Mary knowing he was in the clear. For a moment he thought she had it figured out and he would have to report back to Victor that the jig was up.

"Here's your receipt Mrs, and please the offer still stands," Camden calmly stated careful to not lose his composure.

"Please, call me Mary. After all, I will be seeing more of you over the next five weeks. I will be sure to call you for my impromptu rides. There's something about you that feels so comfortable," Mary blurted out.

Camden quickly jumped out of the taxi and opened the door closest to the sidewalk for Mary to exit. He then proceeded to retrieve her luggage from the trunk, pleased that he would be hearing from her again.

"Can I assist you with these into the hotel?" Camden offered.

"No! No thank you Camden," Mary professed. "I will have the doorman bring them to the concierge. I've been notified by text that they already have me check in. I have a very proficient assistant," Mary explained with a slight hint of sarcasm.

"Well your assistant does sound very efficient, I'm surprised you didn't bring them with you to handle all your day to day activities," Camden said clearly stepping over the line with his comment.

"Pffff, efficient! I don't want efficient. This is exactly why I'm here in Toronto… errrrgg… What I mean is I need and I want to do things on my own for these few weeks. Sometimes I feel like everyone overshadows my every move and decision these days," Mary went off.

"You seem extremely capable of handling people and things all on your own," Camden declared hoping to gain some of her trust.

"I am capable! And I will tell you another thing! I have never needed anyone to help me in life. Not a single person. I have always done it on my own and I wish that the people who love me and are close to me would get that through their heads," Mary stammered.

"Ohhhkaaayyy thaaann," Camden slowly spoke.

"I'm so sorry Camden. It's been a very long day of travel and my head isn't in the clearest of states right now," Mary tried to explain.

"No, really, I get it. No need to apologize. Really, I'm used to this kind of thing," Camden backed out.

Mary waved the doorman over who was patiently waiting her arrival.

"All of the staff at The Four Seasons Hotel had been instructed to wait on Mrs. Mary's every whim," he spoke in a professional tone.

The door man quickly retrieved Mary's luggage and held the hotel door open for her.

"See what I mean? I'm always being taken care of from the protective loved ones in my life. Well I guess this is good bye for now," Mary said extending her hand.

Camden quickly took Mary's hand and gently kissed the back of it in true royalty fashion. Mary couldn't help but stare at the word *hate* carved on his forefingers. He seemed so gentle and kind, unlike someone that advertised hate on their hand.

"I am at your service. You have my card, I look forward to your call," Camden repeated all while imitating a poorly delivered English accent hoping to lighten her mood.

Mary turned and walked through the front entrance of the hotel with the doorman tagging behind her. Camden waited for a moment to see if she turned around to look. His degree in psychology had taught him a few things in life. When he witnessed Mary turn and look back, he instantly knew she would be calling. It was then and only then Camden knew he could return to his car and drive away with confidence.

"She will be calling, and soon," Camden said to the recipient on the other end of his cell phone call.

True to Mary's hotel confirmation text message, her suite was pre arranged and magnificent. The sophisticated suite featured neutral tones with floor to ceiling windows offering a picturesque view of the city. Mary strolled over to the bar area fully stocked with her favourite brand of vodka and a few select bottles of wine. Without hesitation, she walked directly over to the Oval Swarovski Crystal Vodka proudly displayed on a rotating LCD display unit allowing for the Swarovski crystals to glimmer. She grabbed herself a glass and generously poured a liberal amount. Strolling over to the white leather sofa,

Mary kicked off her Louboutin pumps and plopped herself down. Exhausted from her travels she knew she had to call Victor and report her safe arrival. A phone call she was not overly enthusiastic about making but one she knew she needed to do.

~8~

Victor had been pacing his apartment anticipating a telephone call that seemed to be taking forever to come in. He nearly dropped his cell phone when it started to ring. The call from his old school mate he had been waiting for all day finally happened. He needed to make sure Camden came through for him.

"Hello?" Victor answered.

"Hi honey," Mary replied. "As promised, I'm calling to let you know that I've arrived."

"I'm happy you called and equally happy your arrival is safe," he continued. "I'm not even going to ask you about your flight but I presume it was nothing short of a mild heart attack," Victor joked.

"Ha, ha, ha! You're very funny Victor. Surprisingly enough, I managed to keep it together quite nicely. You don't need to worry about me. I've told you before and I'll tell you again that I am completely capable to taking care of myself," Mary stated.

"I know you are but you don't have to try and prove it to me you know," he said.

"I'm not trying to prove anything to anyone. In fact, I'm taking complete charge of my life starting now," Mary proposed.

"What do you mean by that?" Victor asked with concern.

"I know you're not going to like this but I asked you for some space so I can clear my head and I knew you wouldn't have given it to me. I know it's in your nature to be protective of me but sometime I feel that your constant hovering only hinders my ability," Mary tried to explain.

"I, um, hovering?" Victor stuttered.

"Listen! I want to come back to New York a new woman. I want to do things on my terms and by *do things* I mean seek treatment and deal with my emotions on my terms only. I know you try to help in your own kind ways by taking control but really that's not helping at all. It just pushes me further into a reclusive state. Don't you get it? Richard was a huge control freak and didn't allow me to be myself. Although your actions are of a true loving nature, the act behind them is still in a controlling kind of manner," Mary clarified with tears in her eyes.

"Mary..." Victor whispered.

"No! Don't Mary me with your sweet tender voice that has the ability to suck me back into the protective world of the great and powerful Victor," Mary demanded. "I have to do this! I need to repair the Mary I once was and I have to do this solo," she declared.

"Okay Hans," Victor said trying to lighten the conversation a bit.

"Okay, and see? This is exactly why I am doing this. You are not taking me serious," Mary proclaimed.

"I am, I am," Victor pleaded but he couldn't help show some sort of excitement for her. Mary was actually seeking help for her troubles and Victor couldn't be happier. "You know I like to joke around. My foolish and cute boyish ways used to make you laugh."

"Listen! I'm not sure when it was that you stopped taking me serious but you better listen up because I am nothing short of being serious at this very moment," Mary told him turning her tears into slow and sharp words.

"You have my full attention," Victor smugly said.

"Good!" Mary snapped.

The moment of silence was nearly deafening as Victor waited for the next sentence to come through the telephone. He waited with anticipation; sure that Mary was going to tell him she was seeking treatment. His e-mail messenger chimed indicating that he had received an important e-mail message, throwing his concentration away from her.

"I'm turning off this cell phone so you cannot reach me. I want total and complete space to be on my own and get through the next few weeks uninterrupted and without outside influence as to what I should and shouldn't be doing," Mary informed him.

Victor quickly opened his laptop screen to check the urgent e-mail he just received all while trying to absorb the news Mary has sprung on him.

"Turning off your cell phone? Mary, is that really necessary? What if something of an urgent matter comes up and I really need to reach you? How can you just shut yourself off from the outside world like that when you're miles away from home?" Victor asked trying to make sense of it all.

"Because Victor, you can't seem to give me the space that I have asked for over and over. This is the only way I can be sure you're not going to hound me and call every hour or make me promise that I will call you to keep you up to date on my every move," she tried to explain.

Victor felt a sense of relief when he discovered the important e-mail he received was from Camden. The e-mail stated that he had made contact with Mary and that he was confident the first impression was lasting.

"Okay then, I got it. If that is what you feel you need to do than I have no choice but to respect your wishes," he calmly spoke.

Mary knew Victor well enough to know he was only in agreeance because he didn't want to upset her. Their near ten years of marriage proved to be solid but Mary could almost predict Victor's next move before he even could think of it himself.

"Oh, and by the way I will be checking out of this hotel in a few days," Mary indicated with a silent snicker.

"Checking out of your hotel, yup got it and mental note taken," Victor sarcastically stated.

"Clearly you don't think I'm an idiot who doesn't know you will show up at my door unexpected to check up on me," Mary said. "Or even have one of your goons follow me around and report back to you."

"No Mary, I really don't think you're an idiot and I never will," he replied sound defeated.

Victor knew that his good buddy Camden would report back to him on her every move offering great detail of her daily activities and travels. Feeling quite proud that Mary hadn't suspected Camden as a spy and his unobtrusive plan to keep tabs on his wife, he could hardly contain his excitement at the thought of having one up on her. It's in his nature to be aggressive with his planning and equally unique with his ability to keep a strong handle on his personal matters.

"Well then, it's settled! I'm glad I was able to be truthful and upfront with you about this. I've already arranged another cell phone, one that I will use strictly for business. Just a side note Victor, my personal assistant and office do not have my number either. They have been given strict instructions to send an e-mail to me but only if it is of an urgent matter. I will be taking some time away from work and that is all you need to know right now," Mary informed as clear as she could. Knowing Victor like she did, she was certain he would interpret her words like some secret encrypted message was hidden in them.

"Alright honey, please be safe and know that I am here waiting for your return. I've always been on your team and I will always cheer for your success. I love you," Victor uttered as his last words.

Mary ended the call with a simple but sultry, "I love you too."

Sitting back on the white leather sofa, Mary felt a sense of accomplishment and pride. She felt good to be back in charge of her life again which allowed her to let out a sigh of relief. Sipping on her vodka, she wandered into the master bathroom and began to run the water in the oversized jet tub. Soaking in a nice hot bubble bath was exactly what she needed to help her unwind. For the first time in a very long time, she had nowhere to go, no one to see, no appointments to keep. Finally, Mary was able to soak in her own thoughts and not worry about any outside disturbances.

Letting the final clothing item slip from her tense grip, Mary watched as it fell to the floor. Standing naked and peering at the heap of clothing, she wondered how her life had come to mimic a heap of dirty clothing. Her filthy past of sexual deviance and mental torture had soiled her everyday living. Placing one foot into the tub to ensure the proper temperature, Mary climbed in full body, mind and soul. As she lay still in the tub, Mary remembered the shame she had always felt after Richards attacks. She slowly rubbed her hands softly over her skin trying to wash away the impurities that had never shed her soul. Allowing herself to sink back and lower into the warm water, Mary closed her eyes fully aware that the flood of memories were about to drown her conscious mind.

"I'm not afraid of you anymore!" Mary screamed out.

Richard's subtle laugh while sporting a small crooked grin was the first indication of his aroused mood. Mary learned to read his face and understated gestures quickly so she could try and come up with an escape before he really went at her. It took some time to discover his pattern but Mary knew that look for she had witnessed it many times. That cold Christmas Eve night was no different than the others only there was no escape this time. No family to run to, no friends to need her help, no office open to call her in and no client in desperate need of her service. As Mary looked up from the comfort of her couch, she could see Richard walking toward her with that smug little grin and a quiet laugh resonating deep within him. Without any verbal warning, Richard grabbed Mary from the top of her head, ripping at her hair.

"Stop teasing me you little bitch," Richard hissed as he kissed her cheek. His words spewing from his mouth so rapidly and with great force, Mary could feel the little spit splatters land on her face. With an immediate response, Mary wiped the saliva drops from her face. Just as her hand cleared the moist residue off of her right cheek, Richard punched her straight in the face.

"How dare you! Who do you think you are wiping my kiss off your face?"

Richard yanked her head back with such force, Mary couldn't help but whimper. Richard proceeded to lick her entire face making sure she felt every tongue stroke.

"Don't you dare try to wipe it off this time you skanky little twat. I've given you the best of me and this is how you repay me? Do you know how many little bitches want to ride my cock on a daily basis and this is the welcome home treatment I get from you?"

Mary's eyes were blurry, making it difficult to focus on Richard's face. She wasn't sure if her lack of focus was from the punch Richard gave her or if it was her own tears flooding the surface of her eyes. She could feel her legs shaking in terror and her heart was beating out of her chest. Mary was sure Richard would kill her this time and she was terrified. Mary could feel warm liquid slowing trickling down her leg. She quickly realized she was urinating uncontrollably. Her cries became louder and she felt her knees buckle from underneath her. Richard let her fall to the carpet, kicking the side of her torso ensuring she landed face down.

"Why are you doing this to me?" Mary managed to muffle.

"Why am I doing this to you? Why am I doing this to you! Doing what to you?" Richard innocently asked. "Baby, you know you've always turned me on and that you have been the only woman who arouses me beyond the point of control."

"Okay. Let me get up so I can please you like never before," Mary said convincingly; trying desperately to take control of the situation.

"That's my girl," Richard reacted with the very same smirk that started the whole vile episode.

Richard unbuttoned his dress shirt while he watched Mary pick herself up off the floor. He reached for Mary's shirt startling her which made her jump back.

"There you go teasing me again," he said in a playful tone this time.

Richard reached for her again only this time ripping her shirt wide open. He watched as a button went flying across the living room. This seemed to please Richard and his facial expression showed just how much. His thick big hands pulled Mary's bra up exposing her soft breasts. Immediately his thumb and pointer finger started squeezing on her nipples making them erect. With his left hand, Richard grabbed Mary's wrist and vigorously placed her hand on his erect penis forcing her to stroke him up and down repeatedly through his pants.

"Now, now baby, you don't want me getting off too quickly. You said you were going to please me like never before," he reminded her.

"Yes, I'm going to," Mary agreed trying to think of her next life saving move.

Mary quickly dropped to her knees to perform fellatio hoping that was all she needed to do to please his sexual appetite for the evening. Undoing his pants slowly, she wished an escape idea would surface soon. The only reasonable getaway she could think of was trying to please Richards as quickly as she could with minimal torture and damage to herself physically and mentally. With that plan in mind, Mary tried everything she could to speed up the process. She even started to moan and look up at him with what she believed to be sexy eyes that screamed how totally into it she was. With a tight grip on the back of her head, Richard sped up her rhythm pushing his penis down her throat deeper and deeper. Mary gagged and almost threw up. She desperately tried to hide how repulsed she was with him. Displeased with this, Richard pulled himself out of her mouth, slapped her on the cheek with his wet penis and proceeded to mount her from behind.

"I thought you were a better slut than that, My Pretty," Richard whispered in her ear as his sweaty body lay slumped over her back.

Penetrating her vagina, Richard slipped in and out effortlessly.

"I don't know why I even try to get off pounding your pussy," Richard rudely said. "It's so loose now I can't even tell my dick is in it."

"That's not..," Mary started to say.

Richard guided his very hard penis into Mary's anal cavity. He pushed himself so far in, Mary screamed out in pain.

"That's my girl," Richard exclaimed with satisfaction.

"It's hurting me, please stop," Mary pleaded.

"Stop being a baby and lift your ass higher," Richards dismissed.

With a firm grip on Mary's hips Richard slammed himself deeper and deeper into his so called love. With her every whimper and painful cry she made, Richard pushed harder.

"I'm going to give it to you so hard, you're going to split in half bitch," Richard bellowed out from the top of his lungs as he reached his climatic trance.

~9~

Mary jolted upright forgetting she was soaking in her tub. Wrapping her arms around her legs in an upright fetal position, Mary listened intently to ensure there was no one in her suite. It was then, at that moment she realised the importance of getting herself help.

"I'm safe…I am safe…I…am…safe," Mary repeated until she fully accepted the words coming out of her mouth.

Not having Victor there to protect, support and ensure her safety, Mary found herself very vulnerable and lonely.

"I need to call him so he can tell me everything is going to be okay," she said out loud hoping her words resonated truth to her ears.

Stepping out of the cold bath, Mary reached for her towel. She caught a glimpse of her naked body in the foggy mirror. Stopping in mid grab of her towel, she analyzed her shape and posture. She noticed a shift in her skeletal frame even though she was still firm and in good health. Her once very erect and almost militant posture had now shifted. Her shoulders started to curl and her head appeared to hang forward more than she has ever noticed. With a sense of defeat Mary turned away and wrapped her tattered soul with her bathrobe.

"I can't do this anymore," she whimpered as she reached for her cell phone.

Mary made her way into the kitchenette area to make a hot cup of tea hoping to sooth her soul and calm her fears. Reluctantly she started to dial Victor but cancelled the call before it connected.

"What am I doing?" she asked herself. "I can't possibly call Victor and allow him to know how brutally weak I am right now."

The internal voice of reason told Mary that Victor was the perfect person to call during her personal crisis. Victor had always been on her side, her rock and her voice of reason. He was exactly who she should be calling right now. Knowing that she pushed Victor away shamed her deeply and now she wanted nothing more than to be held in his strong and safe arms. Mary dialed his number again, this time allowing the connection to go through.

"Hello? Mary? It's late, is everything okay?" Victor asked with concern in his voice.

"Yes Victor, everything is okay…for now anyway," she stated with mild fear still reverberating in her voice.

"Baby, please take a deep breath and try to keep calm. I can be on the next flight out to help you get through anything you need," Victor assured her.

"Thank you my love," Mary responded gently and with a little more ease. "I really just needed to hear your kind voice. You've always had a calming way about you and it keeps me grounded."

"I'm so very happy to hear you can find solace and comfort within my words," he asserted.

"You've always had that benevolent affect on me. Just like when we first met. You took me under your wing and nurtured my every waking moment. It's now time for me to spread my own wings and learn to do it on my own. I'm not saying I'm not thankful for all that you've done for me but I really do think it's time I get the appropriate care I need," Mary expressed.

"I cannot agree with you more my dear, Victor consented. "I just can't help but want to walk along side with you through your journey. All I've ever wanted was your true love and all I've ever needed was given but there is always that shadow of doubt with you. You could never fully open your heart to me."

"I'm sorry," she whispered. "I really want to give you my whole heart and soul in this marriage and that is exactly why I'm seeking the help I need now."

"I'm with you one hundred percent baby," Victor confirmed. "Your health and mental well being is the only thing I want and need you to concentrate on right now."

"Thank you. Your support and kind words are the only thing getting me through this and I love you full heartily for it," Mary explained.

"Just know there is nothing to be ashamed of. People from all walks of life, all classes, all shapes, ethnic backgrounds go through tough times. Some never seek help and others do. I am so incredibly proud of you for taking the necessary steps needed to get you in a better space. I couldn't love you any more than I do now for showing me your strength," he declared with passion in his voice.

"I really thought I had my life together, you know? I thought that if I could be bigger than my experience and fears. I thought with time I would be able to overcome any weakness and torment I endured," Mary tried to explain.

"I get that approach, really I do Mary," Victor said trying to keep the conversation positive.

"It's just the more I think about it, the more the past keeps creeping into my present," she openly admitted. "What if I just sought treatment years ago when you asked me to? What if I just listened to my internal voice and…"

"You've done nothing wrong Mary. You are the victim here. Please don't torture yourself with all the what-if's," Victor calmly stated. "There is no right answer here. You are taking the necessary steps to better yourself now and that's all that matters at the moment."

Mary's fear and anxiety seemed to calm down during her conversation. Listening to Victor utter kind words without judgement or hostility solidified Mary's trust and love in him. He had always been her rock, her foundation of life and she knew she needed to start recognizing his role in her healing process. She wondered how she became so lucky to have such an amazing and understanding man in her life. Anyone else would have probably left her and her demons behind. But at least now, she was able to assure herself with an apologetic smile, that getting help would allow her to live a normal and productive life again. First thing in the morning she planned to make an appointment with a psychologist who could help her overcome her traumatic past. Victor mentioned to her a while back about a highly recommended psychologist named Dr. Charlie Vasti. Mary wasn't sure where his office was located but she was sure to research him as a starting point.

"I was going to call you with a few recommendations I researched in the Toronto area but I knew you didn't want me interfering," Victor explained to her. My family doctor gave me some names as well. I can pass the list of Doctor's names onto you, and," Victor paused knowing he was smothering her with all of this information. It was too soon to get into great detail over the phone, especially when Mary made it quite clear she didn't want or need his help.

"Let me know how you're doing from time to time," Mary added sensing the hold back from Victor. "I know I've said some pretty hurtful things to you and I apologize to you. My behaviour has been off the wall and I do recognize that but I still feel very strong about getting the help I need on my own."

"If you think it will make a difference in your recovery than I will back away," he agreed.

"I just want to make sure you're all right too." She was instantly sorry those words slipped out of her mouth. She clenched her teeth and waited for Victor's rebuttal.

"I will call once in a while, but not too much. I wouldn't want to crowd your recovery," he truthfully added.

"I'm calling to make a doctor's appointment tomorrow morning. I will call you and fill you in on all the details including when and where so you don't worry." At least it was an excuse to call him. She knew she would need to hear his calming voice of reason periodically. She just didn't want him to know it. After all, she did tell him to leave her alone. She could never go back on such a final statement. Mary was pretty sure her inner weakness would get exposed if she told Victor how much she really needed him. Everything about Victor spoke of his solid character. He always had his life so put together and organized. Mary was positive that his polished lifestyle was second nature to him but Victor would never concede to such a statement. He enjoyed being in charge of his life, and all the people in it but there were days that don't run as smooth as he wished them to.

"Thank you for keeping me informed," he stated.

"I've been such a spoiled brat lately and I'm so thankful to you for being so understanding. I really don't know how you put up with me some days," she admitted.

"You are a beautiful woman Mary, inside just as much as outside. Your beauty resonates all around you, through your mannerism, your smile and your unconditional love for me. It would take a whole heck of a lot more to get me to leave you alone. Besides, you really do need me even if you won't admit to it."

With a slight laugh, Mary agreed with his comment and offered a few choice words before ending the conversation for the evening.

"Thank you for reminding me of that Victor," she whispered. "I love you more than I could ever express."

"I love you too Mary, sleep well my love," he replied.

With those few words, they both ended their side of the call. Victor sat in pure silence for a few moments allowing their telephone conversation to echo through his thoughts a few times. The studio penthouse had grown dark and eerily cold. He wondered if the woman he loved would find solace in her treatment. He also couldn't help wonder if their empty house would find the light and love it needed to become a home. Victor yearned for children and desperately hoped he could have that life with Mary.

Knowing she needed to emotionally heal before starting a family, Victor didn't push too hard to have a child with her but Mary knew his deep desire to start a family. Without standing up, Victor reached over and pulled the cashmere blanket over his body for warmth, imagining it was Mary keeping him warm. Still sitting in the dark, he stared out the window thinking of his one true love.

~10~

The morning air was vastly different in Toronto according to Mary's senses. Although her childhood allergies seemed to dissipate over time, her love of the fresh crisp city air didn't. Her early awakening proved to be a beautiful sight. Looking through the floor to ceiling window while the sun was just rising gave Mary a calming and relaxed start to her day. Knowing she had a difficult call to make, Mary wanted to soak up the day's purity before plunging into her nightmare past. She wasn't dreading the actual phone call to the psychologist, but rather experienced trepidation in having to relive all the horrific details of her torturous past relationship. Mary opened the picturesque window allowing everything the city had to offer to flow into the hotel suite. The soft dewy wind filled the suite rapidly permitting Mary the pleasure of the fresh fall air to awaken her senses. Strolling effortlessly into the kitchenette, Mary plugged the kettle in. Today was the day she would make the most important call of her life, and that call would hopefully put a smile on her face. When her cell phone rang, she jerked at the surprising interruption leaving her soothing ambiance in an instant. The adrenaline rush made her lightheaded so she picked up her cell phone and made her way over to the overstuffed tanned leather lounge chair. While seated, Mary looked at the local number on her display screen. The unfamiliar caller continued to ring. Reluctantly, Mary answered the call, mostly to get the annoying ring tone to stop making racket that early in the morning.

"I've got to change that ring setting," she said out loud just before answering the call. "Hello?"

"Hey there," the unfamiliar male voice responded.

"Hi?" Mary retorted questionably.

"How's it going this morning? Did you get a good sleep in?" the mystery caller asked.

"Yes. Well, somewhat of a restful night," Mary openly admitted.

"I'm glad to hear it because today my new friend, I am treating you to lunch at the most fabulous lunch spots around," he indicated.

"Ummm, I'm terribly sorry but I don't know whom I am speaking with," Mary admitted shyly.

With a nervous chuckle, he quickly reminded Mary about their encounter the previous day.

"I'm so sorry, I really should have said who I was from the get go. It's Camden. The fine young gentleman who drove you to your suite from the airport yesterday," he reminds her.

"Camden! Right, Camden how could I forget," Mary openly admitted feeling a little foolish.

"No worries. I just thought that you might enjoy some company today seeing as it's your first real official day in Toronto," he assumed.

"Right, of course, it is," Mary said convincingly. "Your offer sounds appealing however I'm not exactly sure how my schedule is going to pan out today."

"I completely understand," he agreed. "Please remember that I am at your driving needs for entire day. I'm sure you will need a personal driver to bring you about your business at some point today."

"Actually I do," Mary admitted. "I almost forgot about wanting to be completely clandestine on this journey."

"Your wish is my command," Camden said with complete drollery.

In a boyish undertone, Camden playfully verified a time for pick up and without notice, confirmed a lunch reservation at a swanky restaurant located near Mary's hotel.

"Wow," Mary impressively blurted out while unplugging the whistling kettle. "You are good."

With a full out belly laugh, Camden asked the appropriate question of what it is he's being accused of being good at.

"Taking complete control of my personal affairs," Mary openly accepted. "I have had some pretty impressive assistance that lacked this very talent you acquire so naturally."

"I will wait on your call back for when you need me to take you to your meeting, but please keep in mind that you must break for lunch at some point in your day," he blurted.

"Yes Sir!" Mary sternly said.

"Lunch is tentatively scheduled for one o'clock this afternoon, however if your meeting runs late I can have it scheduled later," Camden said in a professional and convincing tone.

"Perfect! I'm sure I will need a good distraction today," she replied as she started to drift off into another thought.

"Talk to you soon," Camden quickly stated before dismissing the call.

Unsure as to why she felt so giddy, Mary stood up to look at her reflection in the mirror. Resetting the kettle, Mary peered at her reflection in the mirror that was hung above the kitchenette counter. Carefully tilting her head side to side, Mary realized her youthful glow had started to fade. Pulling back on her cheeks with her two hands she wondered how it was she was able to maintain her beauty through all her torment. She found it comforting to know that no one seemed to notice how life's gravity had been pulling at her, leaving her soul feeling broke, heavy and injured.

The sound of the kettle whistling snapped her back into reality. With a hot cup of freshly brewed tea, Mary walked over to her dressing area and flipped through the few outfits she had already hung in the closet. Feeling slightly worn out from her first telephone call, Mary knew she had to place her next call without delay. She researched a few therapist located in her direct area quickly settling on one in particular. Dialing the Doctor's number, she sat on her hotel bed with her teeth clenched waiting for an answer on the other end of her call. To her surprise a female voice-mail recording was what greeted her.

"You have reached the office of Dr. Copeland, licensed psychologist. Please leave your name, phone number and brief message. If you are calling because you are experiencing an emergency, crisis, or require immediate assistance, please hang up and call 911 or go to the nearest emergency room. Please note that

Doctor Copeland is accepting new clients but availability is limited."

Just as Mary cleared her throat, the voice-mail beep sounded throwing her off on her pre-meditated message she practiced in her head so many times before.

"Yes, um hi. My name is Mary and my number is (212)662-2379. I would like to book an appointment with Dr. Copeland. I'm not from this area, well, what I mean is I'm here for about a month. I live in New York but...Oh my, this is not a brief message. Please call me when you get a chance to book an appointment. Thanks."

Fumbling with her phone, Mary nervously repeated her voice-mail message out loud.

"How can a successful woman sound like such a fool," she asked herself.

With no one to answer, Mary decided to forget about the disastrous voice-mail mishap and get on with her day. With a quick call back to Camden, Mary decided to have him pick her up in an hour allowing her some time to put herself together. She could fit a little retail therapy in before heading out to lunch with her new found friend. Yorkdale Shopping Centre ought to do the trick for her. It had been years since she shopped in Toronto. Toronto shopping did not even come close to the shopping choices in New

York but it would have to do. Mary read somewhere that Marciano was having a grand re-opening and she wanted to browse their fall collection. The weather was getting brisk and her constant goose bumps were not just from her past memories. Toronto's fall season was stubbornly known for turning from hot to cold within a day's time.

Instead of gussying herself all up, Mary took advantage of her extra time to do more research on Dr. Copeland. From what she could find, he was a well renowned therapist who specialized in mental and emotional mind function. Although some of his reviews where unfavourable, most were raving on his wondrous ability to help with their problems. She read that Dr. Copeland had been practicing in the Toronto area for nearly ten years but he originated from New York. Mary instantly felt an attachment knowing the doctor stemmed from the same two areas that she had resided in. Perhaps his knowledge in psychology and residential choices would favour her therapy to some degree. Mary found it odd that his last review post was dated back a few years. She chalked it up to being an old forum and closed her laptop with certainty that her choice with this Doctor's was indeed the right one. Not needing to know anymore about him, Mary was certain meeting him would determine her comfort level the best. Getting to know each other face to face was always the best way to establish a comfort level. If he seemed sly and sleek, she would just reach out to a new therapist and start her search over. If he was gentle, kind and understanding to her past encounters she would be more willing to continue with a lasting and committed course of treatment. Only time and the initial meeting would tell.

Just then, Mary's phone beeped indicating a new text message. It was from Camden letting her know he was downstairs for her whenever she was ready to leave.

~11~

As soon as he saw her, Camden jumped out of his waiting car to greet her. He opened the door to the back seat for her as any chauffeur would. His black luxury vehicle screamed privacy with dark tinted windows. The leather interior was noticeably spotless and the car aroma oozed that new car smell.

"Is this a new car Camden? It's not the same one you picked me up in at the airport is it?" Mary asked politely. That day almost seemed like a distant memory even though it occurred nearly 24 hours prior.

"Ya, well no really," was his explanation.

"Okay then," Mary sarcastically uttered.

"Well what I mean is that it is different from the one I picked you up in yesterday but it's not new. Well, new to me," Camden paused.

"It's nice is all I'm saying," Mary reassured.

"Thank you Madame," he joked hoping to change the topic. "Where are you off to today?"

"Considering my appointment has not been confirmed for a specific time, or date for that matter; I am going shopping," she declared.

"Shopping it is! So where would you like to go shopping?" Camden asked.

"Yorkdale please," she informed him in a rather professional tone.

"Yorkdale Shopping Centre it is. You know we could have walked there," he forewarned. "It will actually take longer to get through traffic and park than it would to walk to the Centre."

"Thank you Camden but I do believe I hired you to drive me to my destinations, not advise me on the best mode of transportation," Mary concluded.

"Yes, of course," he uttered. "Please accept my apologies."

"Oh my God! Geesh, I was only fooling around with you," she explained half laughing. "I'm hoping this day relaxes me and lifts my spirits up a bit so no more formalities okay?"

"Oh, okay," Camden said with relief. "For a moment I thought I had really pissed you off."

"No, don't be silly," she giggled. "In fact, today you are going to be my personal shopper and my companion."

"Sounds like you have our day all planned out," he exclaimed with pride. "Don't forget your lunch date too."

"Lunch date? Well I wouldn't go as far as calling it a date. I am married you know," Mary reasserted.

"I know that, I just meant...Well what I should have said is your lunch mate," Camden corrected.

With a girlish smile and a slight chuckle Mary's day seemed to have picked up already. Camden was the exact type of friend she had been looking for. He wasn't possessive and he seemed to understand her need for pure friendship without any strings attached.

"My Mate, we have arrived," Camden joked.

Opening the back door and extending his hand to assist Mary's exit from the car was the first of many kind and friend like gestures Camden offered Mary. They both strolled through the clothing stores arm and arm as if they had been friends for many years. They would exchange glances and looks of both disapproval and approval on items that were being considered for purchase. Their natural correspondence with one another flowed flawlessly and without effort. It was like they were meant to be friends with each other from day one. Mary was more than pleased to have made such a strong personal connection with Camden.

"Maybe this is exactly the type of trip I needed to get my head screwed back on straight," she vowed.

"I wasn't aware your head was crooked," he interjected.

"Well what I mean is I'm having some problems with a few personal things in my life and I'm hoping this trip back home can help ground me," she tried her best to explain without getting into great detail.

"Home?" Camden questions her statement. "I thought you told me that you're here visiting and that you've been here only a few times before."

"Yes, you're right I did say that," Mary defended. "Only I'm not going to tell a perfect stranger all my life's personal details the moment I meet them."

"Of course you wouldn't," Camden agreed with her. "I completely understand that logic."

"I'm sorry if you're offended by that but who knew we would hit it off so effortlessly?" Mary added.

"I'm hungry! All this shopping has made my appetite soar into high gear. What do you say we drop off all our bags in the trunk of the car and go to lunch a little earlier than planned? We can sip on a cocktail and chat more," Camden offered.

"Sounds wonderful to me," Mary easily agreed.

Mary sat in the front seat of Camden's car this time. Feeling very comfortable with her surroundings and the company she was keeping, Mary had no qualms with the informality of riding shotgun. Upon arrival at the restaurant, Camden found it necessary to announce they were at the most new and notable restaurant *Bar Raval,* indicated by *Now* Toronto's food and drink magazine. Hoping to impress Mary a little more, Camden also arranged to have a small bouquet of seasonal flowers be placed on their awaiting table.

"I'm very impressed!" Mary stated.

"It's the beginning of our new found friendship," he contended all while pulling her chair out for her to sit comfortably.

"You know, there are times in my life when I think to myself that I'm truly blessed to have the things I have and the people that surround me. It means the world to me," Mary tried to explain. "But then there are times when I just can't make any sense of what and why things keep coming back to bite me in the butt."

"That, my dear, is a loaded statement," Camden said trying to divert the conversation. "Let's start at hello again."

"Okay. Hello!" Mary said in a soft voice.

"Well not that literally," Camden laughed.

They ordered their starting cocktails when the waitress made her way around. The restaurant's intimate atmosphere made conversation easy and allowed another level of intimacy to grow between the two new friends. Camden's easy going personality made for a refreshing change that effortlessly allowed Mary to open up. She told him about her previous years growing up and living in Toronto and her move to New York when she was trying to build her career as a broker. After a few more cocktails and a bucket of laughter, Mary felt a little more comfortable in sharing some of her past about Richard. Not quite getting into Richard's rigid or savage behaviour but rather her deep imploring love she once had for him. Mary danced around the good times and skipped a few steps past the barbarous acts that scared her crying soul. Camden could easily see past Mary's smile. The wall of strength she held in front of her in an attempt to shield her from her terrifying past was openly visible to him. Like the bold cocktails they were easily consuming, Camden blurted out the only sentence he could think of that could open up the conversation more.

"So is this Richard guy the one you would measure everyone up against?"

Boom! There it was. The one question Mary feared that woke her up out of her tipsy state. A question she asked herself many times before but never really had a solid answer to.

"I never really thought about it that way before," she lied. "He was my first true love but you know what they say about your first love don't you?" she retorted.

"No. What do they say?" Camden flipped the question back at her.

"I don't know!" she laughed while holding her martini allowing it to spill a little. "Oops."

"I'm thinking it's time to order some food," Camden concluded.

"Good idea," she added. "I'm feeling a little loopy. I don't normally drink this many cocktails on an empty stomach and I guess you can guess why," Mary admitted while slurring her words.

Swaying slightly side to side, Mary excused herself to the ladies room. Camden jumped up out of his seat to continue with the gentleman gesture he's portrayed all day but also to help steady Mary from tipping over. As she made her way slowly to the restroom, Camden waved the waitress over to settle the bill. He explained to the waitress that their lunch needed to be cut short due to an unexpected situation and tipped her generously. When Mary returned, she wasn't all that upset to learn that Camden arranged to have her hotel's room service take care of lunch in her suite giving them opportunity to relax and talk in a more quiet and private atmosphere.

~12~

Mary's suite was filled with warm scented air. The essence of her lingering perfume was still evident in the air. Mary's vulnerable state made Camden's invite into her suite that much easier for him.

"Please let me help you get comfortable on the couch here while I take care of room service that should be here any minute," he explained.

"Phew... ok," Mary said all while slumping down onto the couch trying to get the room to stop spinning.

Camden carefully pulled her shoes off and placed them neatly beside the couch. Just when he placed a throw blanket over her legs, he heard knocking at the door.

"I'll attend to the door, you just relax," he instructed.

Mary was feeling very relaxed and quite pleased with the way Camden was taking control, but in a good way. It was nice and welcoming to be waited on from time to time Mary thought. Not having to worry about a single thing is exactly what she needed to ease her mind of all her thoughts. She closed her eyes, if only just for a moment. Enough time to allow the room to stop spinning.

When Camden came back into the sitting area, he found Mary fast asleep on the couch. With not a moment to loose, Camden quickly fetched Mary's cell phone and glanced over her recent text messages. With nothing too enticing to continue the snoop, Camden made his way over to Mary's purse. Surprised by the amount of cash she had in her pocket book, Camden took only a few bills. Just enough to cover the cost of lunch and a bit more keep him happy for the moment.

"Jackpot!" he whispered to himself.

For a very well to do business woman, she sure doesn't keep her bills tidy, he thought. Knowing how successful Mary was with her brokerage firm, Camden didn't anticipate his target to be such an easy catch. For Camden, it was always a rush to pursue a victim who had it all together. Knowing he was collecting secret rewards without his victim's knowledge or without much effort on his behalf seemed to activate his dopamine levels giving him a high that drugs couldn't supply.

Camden's a very intelligent man. His many degrees that once hung on his wall proved that to be true. His love for the wild side always took precedence in his life. He found it more fun and personally rewarding to do things the unconventional way. Camden was successful in his practice, only his personal rewards and profits were not obtained through the traditional methods. Thrill seeking was what always brought Camden to the table quickly. When Camden was younger, his parents would always joke about his wild ways but never feared his antics because he always proved to them that he was still on the right path to a successful adult life. His law studies proved his commitment to building a respectful career but his fast life and easy women always drifted his direction in life. The sudden and tragic accident that took the lives of his parents seemed to straighten him out for a short while. Initially, Camden fell into a depression and turned to alcohol and drugs to ease the pain of his new orphaned life. The constant parties with women and drugs allowed Camden to forget about his pain for awhile. Soon enough, his inheritance was spent and his party friends found somewhere else to hang out. Camden was left with nothing and he knew it was time to start all over again, and he did.

With Mary still asleep, Camden left her suite as quiet as he could making sure the door behind him closed completely. He knew exactly what he needed to do next and it would be perfect for his next planned outing with Mary.

When Mary finally woke up a few hours later, she could still feel the effects of the alcohol she consumed. Slightly confused, she got up off the couch and wandered over to her cell phone that was sitting on the kitchenette counter. She noticed the untouched food there as well and thought better of it to just leave it sit there. After all, she wasn't even sure how long it had been sitting out. Based on the sky colour and lack of sun shining, Mary could only assume she slept for a few hours. Indeed, when Mary observed the time on her cell display, she knew her assumption was correct. Surprisingly, she felt somewhat refreshed and less anxious minus the slight pounding still resonating in her head. A round of drinks seemed to be what the doctor just might have ordered after all. It had been years since Mary allowed herself to indulge in an afternoon of careless activities and countless cocktails. Her new found freedom from her over scheduled appointments and demanding clients felt liberating and refreshing. It felt good to be out socializing, laughing and being mindless of responsibility and expectations. Mary opened her window and stood with her arms stretched out to her sides, breathing in the cool fall air. Perhaps a mental health day was really all she required to get a better grip on her constant visions of her haunting past. After all, she hadn't even thought of Richard all day. Feeling rather giddy and impressed with her current upbeat mood, Mary decided a few more cocktails where in order. Not wanting to make the same mistake as earlier today, she knew she must eat first. Making her way downstairs to the hotel restaurant would be her first priority.

The lounge was beautifully decorated with the season's colours and masterfully crafted flower arrangements strategically placed around the room creating focal points and a warm ambiance. Mary chose an empty table that boasted the perfect and impressive view of Yorkville Avenue. If there was anything Mary enjoyed doing by herself, it was people watching. She found people to be strangely enticing with how they act and react to situations and scenarios. Her street level seating choice gave her ample opportunity to observe the early evening foot traffic. Mary gracefully ordered an assorted terrine along with an impressive choice of a vintage red wine to start. She wanted to be careful not to over indulge, especially because she was on her own. Mary was alone, by herself, unescorted and feeling rather lonesome. She realized she had never been unassisted in life before. There had always been someone there with her to walk through life with. It hadn't always been a pleasing road to travel but a road with companionship nonetheless. Just as Mary sat comfortably contemplating her friendship choices and the repercussions that followed, her uncontrollable and interfering recollection of her Richard days came pouring through. Not wanting to fall apart in the swanky lounge, Mary quickly occupied her thoughts with her earlier encounter with Camden. He was the perfect distraction for her, exactly what she needed. Her fun filled day of shopping and socializing was what her soul seemed to crave even though she felt rather embarrassed that she drank too much. Reminiscing about the day's activities had Mary thinking she should place a call to Camden to let him know she was okay. Thanking him for being such a gentleman and getting her back to her suite was something she should have done the moment she woke up. With that thought, Mary dialed his number from her cell.

"Hello?" he answered.

"Hey! Camden?" Mary questioned.

"Yes, it is he," he responded.

"It's Mary" she stated.

"Mary! Yes, how are you?" he asked with concern.

"I'm fine, just fine," she answered. "Hey listen, I'm really sorry for what happened earlier," she explained.

"Don't even worry about it Mary," he assured her.

"I do worry about it Camden," she continued. "It's not my normal behaviour to pound back cocktails pre lunch hour and then pass out."

With a slight chuckle, Camden expressed his lack of concern for her behaviour and promised not to hold it against her.

"What a relief," Mary declared. "I want to make it up to you."

"There really is no need to make anything up to me Mary," he assured her. "It's nothing we all haven't done one or two times in our life."

"One or two times?" Mary expressed. "People do this more than once?" she joked.

"Believe it or not, I just did it last week. Clearly it wasn't planned but sometimes our judgement gets a little clouded and we forget how to act responsibly."

"Responsible I was not!" she added.

"Let's not make a big deal about it and chalk it up to a little mishap," he bargained.

"I like your way of thinking," Mary admitted. "My whole life I've always tried to do the right thing and follow all the right rules. Really, just to please the people around me I guess. It feels really good to not have to do that once in a while."

"Nothing ventured, nothing gained!" he continued.

"Hey listen," Mary said. "I'm at d/Bar in the lounge at my hotel having something to eat. Would you like to join me?"

"I was not expecting that, but yeah! Sounds great," Camden accepted with great excitement in his voice.

"Okay then, I'll see you soon?" Mary asked.

"How soon is now," he exclaimed. "I happen to have a very special something for you too and I am positive this something is going to put you in complete relax mode."

With a nervous laugh Mary couldn't help but wonder what he could have possibly got for her.

"A spa retreat package?" Mary childishly guessed.

"You'll find out soon enough, eager one," he claimed ending the phone call.

Mary could feel her anticipation escalate with every waiting moment. She could never resist a good surprise.

~13~

An hour nearly passed when Mary couldn't contain her curiosity anymore so she did what any other over anxious person waiting on someone would do. Mary took her phone out and sent Camden a text message. Just as she hit the send button, she heard a familiar voice.

"Patience is not your virtue I take it," Camden uttered.

Standing to greet him eye to eye, Mary explained that her need to know what gifts were awaiting her definitely overrode her better judgement on time etiquette. They hugged one another with a friendly reception. Mary couldn't help but catch a whiff of his delicate but seductive cologne. She wasn't sure why she felt an attraction to him at that very moment but decided to brush it off and offer him a seat at her table. Mary guessed the two glasses of wine she'd consumed was already having an effect as she pulled a chair out for Camden.

"Please, join me," she concluded.

"Thank you Mary I will," he accepted. "It's nice to see you out and looking so beautiful after an afternoon of…well who are we kidding right? This afternoon didn't end so great did it?" Camden inquired.

"No, no it didn't," Mary interrupted. "I thought we conceded that we were not going to make a big deal about it?"

"Relax My Angry Grasshopper," Camden jokingly said. "Wow, you really do need to slow it down a tad."

"I'm not sure why I'm getting so defensive?" Mary tries to explain. "It's been a long day and really I just had something to eat, a few drinks to help me relax and now some pretty great company. What more can a woman ask for?"

"Well…I could think of a few things," Camden snickered with a slight tilt of his head.

"Are you making a pass at me?" she blatantly asked while offering a tender smile and a childish laugh.

Mary could feel her heart starting to race. Why was she enjoying this innocent flirting? His scent and mannerism seemed to draw her into his slightly open arms. She could feel herself drawing closer to him as her arm extended out and touched his.

"At the risk of sounding precocious I believe it is you who is flirting with me," Camden pointed out making his inner thoughts now public.

"No! I don't…I didn't," Mary stumbled for words now feeling uncomfortable and awkward.

Camden knew all too well that he had already started crushing on Mary from the very moment he placed eyes on her. He almost felt like he should apologize for his honest simulation of her actions toward him but he didn't want to bolster any more uncomfortable table talk. He didn't even want to recognize his budding feelings for her. He had a job to do, a mission of sorts and he would be damned if he strayed from his original task.

"Are you married?" she asked trying desperately to change the subject to a more sophisticated conversation between two friends.

"Yes, I was," his voice ascended as he tried hard to keep the thoughts from trailing back into his past memory.

"You're divorced now?" Mary pursued.

"No, I'm widowed," Camden said with a tremendous amount of pain emanating from his voice.

Mary instantly felt his sorrow and pushed her chair next to his. She wrapped her arm around his shoulder in a desperate attempt to console him. Her action deemed futile when he continued to tell her about his wife's tragic car accident. It was a story he painfully knew all too well. He replayed the vision of the accident over and over in his head as if it was on automatic repeat. Still to this day it haunted his thoughts on a regular basis. Self medicating numbed the pain for a short while but eventually the sorrow and heart break seeped through stronger than ever. Camden graduated to stronger narcotics aiding his dangerous slope into depression.

"I'm so deeply sorry Camden, I didn't know," Mary tried to soften his pain. She could see the pain pouring out of his eyes with every word he spoke. "I didn't mean to pry into your personal life," she explained instantly regretting her probing questions.

"It's okay, you didn't know," he stated trying to pull himself together. It was abundantly clear his pain was still very real and raw.

"If you ever want to talk about it I'm here for you," Mary offered, as any friend would.

"Thank you Mary. I never had the chance to talk about it with anyone before. I've always just held it in and tried to push the tragedy deep inside me. Bury the wound and hope it weakened over time," Camden reflected.

"Do you want to order another drink and talk more?" she innocently asked.

"I've tried just about everything else to numb the pain so yes, more drinks sounds great right about now," he denoted.

After ordering another round, Mary wondered if she was getting herself in a little too deep. She doubted that talking about the hurt, anger, fear, tragedy, weakness and sorrow really was the answer; or whether it could it be the start of the healing process? Mary remained so closed lipped about her Richard days, perhaps that was the reason she had never fully been able to put it in the past forever. Victor often offered to talk about it but Mary's shame and guilt continually ruled her decision to not open up to him, or anyone else for that matter. Opening up and talking about her troubles was the reason she came back to Toronto. Her only reason to be in Toronto was to make an appointment with Doctor Copeland and start talking about what continued to tear her up inside, only Dr. Copeland hasn't returned her call yet.

Clearing his throat to speak, Camden started to tell Mary about the accident that took his wife.

"It's been almost eight years since the accident happened," he started. "It was dark and raining. The start of fall had just arrived and the trees where full of colour. It was especially picturesque that year but the weather was already morphing into winter at a quicker pace than years past. That night in particular was a stormy night with heavy wind gusts and multiple lightning strikes. The storm came in from nowhere. I was hanging out with some of my poker friends while Adrianna took a car service with her best friend Gwen into Barrie. I had arranged a weekend getaway for her at a remote spa. It was an early present for her to relax and rest before becoming a first time mom and me a father." Camden's sipped on his scotch seemingly unaffected by the streams of tears rolling down his face.

"The night was young and I was with all the guys feeling pretty good at this point. My phone rang a few times but I guess with all the music and noise I didn't hear it. Gwen did all she could to try and get in touch with me that night but I just didn't hear my cell ringing. Adrianna and Gwen where laughing it up and planning the nursery details when the limousine they were riding in swerved across the highway, bounced off the median, hit a light pole and rolled onto the driver's side into a ditch at the side of the highway. I guess the driver swerved to miss another car and lost control, but there was speculation that the driver could have been checking a text message. Gwen managed to check on Adrianna before searching for her cell phone to call for help. After a brief struggle to locate the cell that flew out of her purse on impact, Gwen dialed 911 with her unsteady and bloodied fingers." The memory of it all came flooding back to Camden. Visibly shaken up, he continued without pause. "The emergency dispatch tried to locate the crash site because Gwen was unaware of their current location. She struggled at times to catch her breath and repeatedly asked the paramedics to come as quick as possible. Gwen was sure the driver was killed on impact but thought she could still feel a slight pulse on Adrianna wrist. Despite the emergency operator instructing Gwen to stay on the line, she hung up and frantically tried to reach me. I didn't answer, I couldn't hear the cell ringing over the noise," he openly cried.

Mary was unaware of the torment, pain and guilt Camden carried with him. He always appeared to have it together. She guessed that the word hate tattooed on his hand had everything to do with his regret. How was it that she didn't see the suffering in him before now? She started to feel rather selfish and guilt ridden for only thinking of her own problems. Camden's heartache and devastating loss was clearly a catastrophic event that would remain a part of his life's memories forever.

"I just kept on with my night playing poker and drinking with the guys completely unaware of the wreckage that just took place," he sobbed.

"It's not your fault Camden," Mary tried to comfort him.

"It is my fault. It's my fault that I drank too much that night and couldn't get to the hospital on time to say goodbye to my wife and unborn child. It is my fault that I chose my friends and gambling rather than driving my wife and her best friend to the resort myself. It is my fault that I arranged the stupid spa retreat in the first place. Why didn't I just do something local for them? Why didn't I hire a registered massage therapist to come to the house for a relaxing night? Why did things have to be that way?" he mourned.

"Oh Camden," Mary empathised while hugging him to try and console him.

"The limousine driver was killed instantly and Gwen sustained some serious injuries but managed to overcome them. Adrianna was still breathing and had a faint pulse when the air ambulance arrived. I know she was fighting hard to stay alive for me and our baby. She fought until the end, with every last bit of strength; until her very last breath. The doctors did everything they could but she and our baby boy slipped into sweet peace just moments before I arrived," he wept.

Crying herself, Mary tried to keep control of her emotions as best as she could. As she listened to Camden tell his story, she watched him relive that painful night and it was that very moment she truly understood how deeply saddened he was. Mary was all too familiar with reliving painful memories over and over again only watching someone else go through it gave new meaning to the buried pain she carried through the years.

"Camden, please don't punish yourself for this tragic loss. There is no possible way you could have predicted or changed the outcome of that evening. I've learned a few things in life and one of them is giving permission to let go of painful events that happen in life in order to heal," she preached knowing all too well she wasn't practicing her own advice. "The hate tattoo on your hand, does it have anything to do with the loss of your wife?" she courageously asked.

"I've let go. I tattooed the word hate across my fingers because it's how I was feeling at the time. I had a lot of built up hate and anguish for the driver that killed my wife. It's been a long road and I'm still trying to forgive myself but I will never forget. They say the limo driver was occupied by a text message he just received on his cell. The police report says that's the reason for the crash but I know better. That other driver coming the opposite way was the reason the limo driver swerved, I'm sure of it," Camden insisted.

"Why don't we settle up the bill and head back to my suite for a while. The night is still young and frankly I'm not that interested in leaving you alone after all you've just told me," Mary professed.

"You're a very kind woman Mary. How is it that I managed to make such an amazing friend with tremendous strength and understanding?" Camden asked.

"Life has a funny way of connecting people together in times of need I guess," she said. "I'm far from having the strength and understanding you may think I have."

"I'll take care of the tab. It's the least I could do for your generous invitation tonight and your remarkable ability to listen. I hope one day I can find the strength and courage you exhibit," he professed with very a sincere look of appreciation.

"Flattery will get you everything," she replied trying to lighten up the mood.

"Oh, and don't forget your gift," Camden said picking up the parcel and handing it to Mary. "It will be the perfect excuse to indulge in total relaxation complete with a positive affirmation to repeat over and over again until you finally reach that highly anticipated gemstone at the end."

"Wow! That sounds enticing and slightly erotic," Mary confessed.

Pulling the wrapped package from Camden's hands, Mary started to open the gift.

"No, no, no!" Camden repeated with an innocent tug back at the parcel. "The gift is meant to entice complete euphoria and you wouldn't want to exercise that type of joyous activity in the middle of a restaurant."

"Mr. Camden! You have my curiosity peaked. Let's get out of here and back to my suite quickly so I can open this excitement you call a gift," she suggested.

It was that moment Mary realized that she didn't even know Camden's last name. How was it that she could already be privileged to know such intimate parts of his past but not know his full name?

"Or get the excitement started," he jabbed with a sleek but piercing look directly into Mary's eyes.

~14~

Arriving at Mary's suite couldn't come soon enough for Camden. Already a few drinks into the night, he started to feel some serious attraction to Mary. Knowing she was married was about the only thing that stopped him from making his signature pick up move. Not only was she married, she was married to his friend Victor, who happened to be paying him handsomely to make sure Mary stayed safe. Victor made it abundantly clear to Camden that under no circumstances was Mary to engage in any activities that could put her into harm's way. Camden accepted the responsibility knowing full heartedly that he was not the same man Victor once knew. The death of his wife and unborn baby boy changed him in ways that other people just didn't and couldn't understand. The sympathy poured in from all over the map but nothing seemed to help heal the gushing hurt he felt from deep inside. The overflowing emotions he kept buried inside had nowhere to escape, up until he met Mary.

Mary handed Camden a drink which seems to snap him out of deep thought.

"Where were you just then?" she asked.

"In a far off land where everything is perfect," he retorted.

Mary placed her glass on the coffee table and excused herself in order to get into something more comfortable. From the bedroom, she asked Camden if he wanted a bath robe to lounge around in so they could hang out comfortably on the couch. Camden politely refused her offer mainly because he was not completely sure he would be able to control his growing emotions around her much longer.

"I better not Mary," he confessed. "It's getting a little late and I shouldn't keep you up much longer."

"Don't be silly," she replied exiting the bedroom in lounge pants and a t-shirt holding a crisp white bathrobe clearly provided by the hotel.

"I really shouldn't Mary, but thank you for asking," he countered.

While standing up to go retrieve Mary's unopened gift, Camden caught a breathtaking whiff of her freshly applied perfume. Unable to control himself, he took Mary's hand and thanked her again for allowing him to open up to her.

Still holding hands, Mary candidly admitted that it was somewhat therapeutic to her as well. She rubbed the letter H carved into his forefinger wishing his pain away.

"There are many things I wish I could tell someone about the happenings that have occurred in my life too so I can tell you with certainty that it was my great honour to have you open up to me with such intimate and personal emotion," Mary revealed.

Acting puzzled by her statement but secretly knowing her truths, Camden decided to take this moment and move into a full embrace. He could feel her tender body pressed up to his and it felt very good.

"Sometimes a warm squeeze is the organic medicine our souls need to keep us from becoming completely toxic," he stated.

Still holding onto Mary's body, Camden reached into his pocket and pulled out his cell phone. Feeling the movement and shift in body position, Mary attempted to pull out of the hug.

"Please just one moment longer," Camden requested.

Mary was happy to oblige to his request at this point. His warm mannerism and touching story of how he lost the only people in his life deserved more than just a minute hug for comfort. Hoping he felt comfort in the innocent embrace, Mary squeezed a little tighter while closing her eyes and wearing a slight smile. Enjoying her embrace, Camden took advantage of the warm moment between them. It was the perfect opportunity to capture their embrace for he wasn't sure when he would get another chance. Without her knowledge, he secretly snapped a picture of them in a full embrace, but when Mary's cell phone started to ring, it quickly ended their personal moment.

"What perfect timing!" Camden blurted out.

While digging through her purse to find her cell phone, Mary questioned Camden's timing comment.

"What I mean is perfect timing for you to take your phone call because I need to step out into the other room and check some messages that were left for me earlier tonight," he confessed.

Feeling confident, Camden made his way into the kitchenette area. A feeling of self-righteousness was not a new trait to him. In his younger years when life had everything to offer him and his parents would see to it; Camden would often push the limits without regard. A feeling he never got tired of or wanted to give up on. It was life's unfortunate turn of events that made him angry and bitter. His self worth was crushed and bent. Life dealt him a raw wound that was too deep to heal and he wanted everyone and anyone to know the same feeling he was struggling with. If only Victor took the time to do his research and stopped believing in a world that was filled with good trusting people, Camden would have never had the opportunity to meet up with Mary. An opportunity to heal himself of his own hollow and empty heart all while delivering a very real message to the over privileged and extremely wealthy people who think they can hire their way around true happiness.

Taking out his cell phone, Camden deemed it to be a perfect time to update Victor on his beloved wife's well being. He comprised his text with a simple message informing Victor that Mary was doing just fine and was in good hands. With that quick note, he attached the photo of Mary and himself in a full embrace and hit the send button.

"Sorry to keep you waiting Mary," he announced upon his arrival back into the sitting area where Mary looked irritated. "I didn't think I was gone that long. Are you okay?"

"I'm fine," she muttered.

"I know well enough not to push when a woman tells you that she's fine," Camden said.

"It's not you," she softened. "I've asked my husband Victor over and over again to give me some space while I'm on this trip and he hasn't. That was him checking in on me…again…for the second time today."

"I'm sure he's just worried about you," Camden tried to sound concerned.

"You know what? That's what he tells me! He's concerned for me, like I can't take care of myself," Mary started to explain. "I already threatened to change my cell phone number before I left New York so he couldn't hound me while I was here. He promised he wouldn't but he has! It's time I stand up for myself so I just changed my cell phone number."

Still holding her cell with an angry clench, she sent her new number to Camden so he would be able to recognize when she was calling him for a ride. A phone number she had previously arranged for before she even left New York. She was hoping to not have to resort to this plan B of telephone number changing but Victor gave her no alternative.

"Good for you! Standing up for what's right in your life," he smugly told her.

"I don't get why men think they can control their significant other and get them to live their lives as only they see fit," she expressed.

"That's a rather vague statement, but I'm going to go with it because I really don't want to piss you off right now," he said half joking.

"It's not you who has pissed me off," Mary retorted.

"Well that makes me feel better," Camden admitted with a smile. "I know what will make you feel better instantly."

"Please, bring it on," Mary said with hope.

"Well, technically I've already brought it but you haven't opened it yet," he stated.

"That's right! My gift you brought me. I've been anxious all night wondering what it could possibly be," Mary giggled.

"How about you open your gift, and I will take you up on the offer to get into that very comfortable looking bath robe," he suggested.

"That sounds perfect," Mary agreed.

Without hesitation, Camden picked up the robe and headed to the master bedroom. After a quick glance around the room, he strategically placed his garments next to Mary's that were already tossed at the end of the bed. Camden made sure his cell phone was still on the silent mode and took a picture of the clothes careful to include his naked legs resting leisurely beside them. Mary knocked on the half open door and waited for her approval to enter the bedroom.

"No need to knock Little Grasshopper," Camden laughed. "I am decent."

"Your gift is perfect, thank you," Mary said with genuine gratitude. "How is it you guessed my peaceful place is soaking in a warm bath by candlelight?"

"Isn't it everyone's peaceful place?" he retorted.

"If it isn't, it should be," Mary conceded.

"I am going to run you a very hot bath, light this candle and get you a glass of wine to sip on," Camden told her with authority. He immediately got up off of the bed and went straight into the master bath. The sound of the water filling up the jet tub soothed any anxiety Mary might have had. Camden hoped the sweet smell of the cherry blossom bath balm would sooth her body aches and calm to her over active imagination. The bath was exactly what she craved. Camden breezed past Mary with a smug smile and fetched a cold glass of white wine from the kitchenette fridge for her to bring into the bath. In the mean time, Mary undressed and wrapped herself with a warm towel. Climbing back onto the bed, she proceeded to make herself comfortable while she waited on her much needed bath. When Camden returned to the bedroom where he found Mary comfortably resting and surprisingly relaxed.

"You look so relaxed I'm not sure you even need the bath I'm preparing for you," Camden joked while handing Mary her chilled glass of wine.

"Cheers to you Mr. Camden for making this night happen," Mary added while toasting her glass against his.

"I have one more little surprise for you My Little Grasshopper," Camden added.

"More surprises? I'm listening," Mary said wearing a big smile of approval.

"Calm down Grasshopper, this surprise is only for me," Camden admitted.

"Okay, I have two questions for you. First why do you keep calling me Grasshopper? My second question is why only for you?" she inquired.

"I call you My Grasshopper for many reasons Mary. The short version is because I can see that you carry attributes of happiness, good health, good luck and virtue according to Chinese symbolism," Camden told her.

"I think you are reading me totally wrong," Mary said while laughing. "What is the long version?"

"The long version will be kept for another time because you my dear need to get into the bath before the water gets cold," Camden instructed.

"Right, I almost forgot about the bath," Mary admitted. She gracefully strolled into the master bathroom letting her towel drop to her feet as she climbed into the bubbly tub. Soaking up all the warmth and wonderful aroma, Mary slid deeper into the water allowing the bubbles to moisten the back of her coiffed hair. "I almost let you off the hook without answering the second question," Mary yelled out from the tub.

Camden strolled into the bathroom holding a pencil thin rolled marijuana cigarette. Casually waiving the joint around in one hand and a lighter in the other, Camden smugly sat on the edge of the tub allowing the bottom half of his robe to open ever so slightly.

"Which one of these surprises do you want me to light first," Camden playfully asked.

"Oh my God, you brought a blunt," Mary said trying to contain her laughter.

"What! Will it be relaxation overload?" Camden asked.

"No not at all. I haven't touched a joint since high school," she admitted.

"If you're willing to go retro high school then I will too," Camden professed.

"Let's do it," Mary agreed.

Camden was surprised to hear Mary agree to smoking pot with him. Everything he knew about her indicated a polished and perfectly fine tuned character. Mary never engaged in shady activity that could remotely tarnish her reputation personally or professionally. Camden was instantly curious, wanting to see how far he could push the boundaries with her.

"Pass it here, don't be a hog," Mary quickly said eager to take a puff.

"A hog? Really? Don't be Miss Grabby Pants," Camden rebutted in a childish tone.

As Mary leaned back in relaxation on the tub wall, Camden couldn't help but stare in amazement. Her beautifully toned body glistening with moisture just as he pictured it in his head all night long during their diner drinks together. It took great restraint for him not to reach out and touch her silky wet arm. He wanted to breathe it all in at the moment and never let the image go. He watched as the bath suds slowly slid down her youthful breasts exposing her nipples. Without hesitation, Camden let his towel drop to the ground and jumped into the bath with her. Fully expecting retaliation for his action, Camden was pleasantly surprised when Mary adjusted her legs to rest on top of his without a word.

"I know what you're thinking," Mary stated.

"If you knew what I was thinking then you would just sit up and kiss me right now," he retorted.

"No, that's not what I meant but now I know what I was thinking was way off the mark," she snorted while puffing another drag from the joint.

"Now look who's being a hog!" Camden said while reaching for the blunt, careful not to wet it with his damp fingers.

"Isn't this nice just to be carefree and not have to worry about what intentions are expected of you? Don't you think that everyone in the world should just be as they should? Why can't we just co-exist globally without having to please everyone around you one hundred percent of the time? Is it really that difficult to allow oneself the freedom of expression without having to perform some kind of miracle to ensure everyone happiness? Mary rambled.

"That's a whole lot of deep questions you just spewed out and frankly I'm not sure I have any of the right answers for you," Camden replied. "I think we should just do whatever it is in life that makes us happy at the moment. You know, like smoking this joint," he added while giving it back to Mary.

"I think you're right. Too many times in my life I've conceded to what everyone else has wanted and what makes everyone else happy. What about what makes me happy?" she revealed.

Mary stood up gracefully revealing her entire naked body without shame or embarrassment. Camden instantly noticed her remarkable beauty but also took notice of a large white scar on her lower back. He could tell from the fading and colour of the wound that it was from some time ago. Curious by nature and from his recent high he decided to enquire about it. Camden instantly noticed Mary's retraction when he did finally mention it. Now standing with a towel tightly wrapped around her as if trying to hide, Mary changed the subject and challenged Camden to a race to see who could get dressed the fastest. Mary's years of being in unwanted situations allowed her to master the art of how to change the subject without too much fall back. This was one conversation she wasn't sure she wanted to be open about. The physical scars left by Richard where unwelcoming but nothing compared to the emotional scars she still wore.

Camden leaped out of the bath without a second thought in order to accept Mary's challenge. Careful not to slip on the wet ceramic floor, he made a mad dash to get into the master bedroom before Mary. While his attempt was almost successful, Mary beat him to the bed allowing just enough time and room for Camden to playfully push Mary on top of the bed. Laughing at the instant replay in her mind, Mary reminded Camden of his nude streak through the hall into the bedroom. They both laid on the bed, side by side in full giggle mode recapping Camden's naked pounce.

~15~

New York City was always a few degrees colder at night, especially in the fall. Victor often stayed at work later in the colder months but this night was different. After not being able to reach his wife he grew increasingly worried. Victor made his way back to their apartment where he hoped he could think more clearly. He grew increasingly lonely without Mary at his side. Mary had grown so distant from him and he felt so trapped in not being able to help her. He knew she wanted her space while away in Toronto but he never imagined she would cut him off completely. He also knew she was very angry at him for checking in on her periodically but he never dreamed she would change her cell number. Changing her cell number made him wonder if she moved hotels too. Victor didn't want to risk finding out. He had to give her a little more space just as she asked but he couldn't shake the feeling that she was in danger. Mary wasn't known to do anything radical and besides, he had his old school friend Camden checking in on her.

Knowing Camden was with her helped Victor feel a little more comfortable. He poured himself a shot of bourbon and settled onto the couch. His long lean legs rested on the ottoman exposing his hairy lower legs and bare feet. With his slippers tucked neatly beside him on the floor he opened his laptop that was nestled beside him on the couch. Not sure what he was going to look up, he started researching the city of Toronto. Partly because finding out more about Toronto helped him feel closer to Mary but mostly because he needed something to keep his mind off of his loneliness. Mary was originally from Toronto so naturally he wanted to know more about the origins of her childhood neighbourhood. Knowing his old schoolmate Camden lived in Toronto for quite a while placed research on the city higher on his priority list. Living in New York his entire life, Victor couldn't imagine what life in a smaller city could offer anyone. New York was filled with life and attractions, entertainment and pizzazz at anytime of the day. Why would anyone want to live anywhere else?

Victor didn't find out much more than he already knew from traveling to Toronto a few times with Mary but his research did manage to pass a few hours of his time. He closed his laptop and gazed out the penthouse window turning his attention to the storm brewing from afar. The night sky was darker than most October nights with the clouds covering most of the night's stars. The thin blanket of lights emanating from the city skyline was not unusual to witness but the increasing strong winds that where showing potential for torrential rainfall was. With Halloween fast approaching, Victor wondered if Mary would make it back to celebrate his favourite holiday. Every year they dressed up with matching costumes and this year Victor had the best costume of all time planned for them. He already ordered the costumes a few months ago and thought the idea to be brilliant. They would be sure to win the office contest showing up as Bonnie and Clyde from the 1967 classic crime movie. Victor secretly practiced his gun holding stance and mastered wearing his brimmed fedora tilted on just the right angle giving him the proper gangster look. His tapered grey pantsuit would slightly mimic his everyday attire but with Mary at his side sporting her properly coiled scarf, beige skirt suit and matching hat, she would surely complement the entire ensemble. In previous years, they dressed as bacon and eggs, Tim Horton's and Starbucks Cups, Frankenstein and his bride as well as Popeye and Olive cartoon characters. Halloween had always been Victor's favourite time of year over any other celebration. It's the one time of year he could completely let loose and forget his everyday strict schedule and demanding lifestyle. Dressing up into something fun and playful always appealed to his ever changing alter ego. The transformation and character change allowed Victor to become someone or something else, even for just a few hours. It was always a welcoming break from his everyday routine. His newly founded Halloween Gala for the Homeless and Hungry would not be the same without his wife by his side. They started the charity together last year. Naturally they should both attend the second annual Gala together. This year he wanted to bring more awareness and change to the stereotype of homelessness. He knew by fundraising with Mary, together they could bring the change and extra attention the Gala needed. He was almost desperate to have Mary with him this year in particular. The need to transfigure their lives and be able to give back to their community was brewing for some time. Victor just couldn't shake that wrenching feeling deep within the pit of his stomach that Mary needed more out of life than what he was currently giving her. He felt Mary slowly slipping away from him only he didn't know how to throw her a life preserver this time. He couldn't seem to save her from her emotional drowning and it scared him. Victor had always been her life raft, her rescuer and voice of reason. How was it that he had failed her this time? She was so broken and emotionally wounded when they met. It took many years of him proving his love, offering comfort, showing strength and giving her stability that allowed her the ability to move on from her tortuous past. So why now after almost ten years of marriage is it not working anymore? Why is it that she needed to get away from him to heal? All of this didn't matter right now anyway. She had Camden to watch over her and keep her safe. Camden was a good friend to Victor back in law school. The death of his parents caused a setback in his career path but after some much needed healing and time, he was able to bounce back, or so Victor thought. He left law school to pursue a career in psychology. After Camden completed his degree, Victor lost touch with him for a while. Their close friendship slowly drifted apart. Their career choices and paths didn't allow them to spend much time together. Camden moved to Toronto where he started his own psychology practice and Victor remained in New York where his law career was already booming. When Victor learned Mary would be visiting Toronto for a short visit, he did what any loving and concerned husband would do. Reconnecting with Camden on social media and arranging for him to watch over the love of his life was the perfect plan to keep her safe. It was the right thing to do, even if Mary was completely oblivious of his arrangement.

It has only been a short time since Mary's departure to Toronto but it already felt like a lifetime to Victor. He poured himself a second shot of bourbon, a double this time. After the rough week at work and his love out of town, Victor found himself more alone than he had ever been in his life. Drinking his sorrows away had never been an option nor had he ever tried to immerse himself in a dependence that could ultimately lead him to the loss of who he stood for in life. Victor had always been an advocate of what was right and just. His belief in equality and keeping a level head in everything he did in life was always important to him. It's what made him one of the best defense lawyers around New York. Despite his better judgement, he once fell into some radical peer pressure when he was out with his school alumni friends. Lucky for him, Mary never found out about his onetime mistake a few years back. Mary was away on business when his law partner Barry invited him out for dinner and drinks. Barry was known as the quiet one in the office. Standing only five feet nine inches, he was considered average height. His light brown hair matched his equally boring eye colour. He was not an ugly man but not an overly handsome fella either. Back in University, he was known as hairy Barry. Rumours circulated that a girl he tried to get with was so grossed out by the abundance of body hair that she threw up all over him during oral sex. Of course being immature guys, his group of friends never let him live it down. Since then, Barry always kept a low key and didn't have much to say to anyone outside of the courtroom. His lack of social skills never hindered his fierce and sharp wit when it came to settling court cases. He was one of the best out there and his success rate of winning cases proved it.

There were a whole group of old school friends attending the dinner party that evening. Victor was informed through company e-mail that it would be a class reunion of sorts. He didn't think much of the innocent invite and Mary was away, so he agreed to attend. Victor was rather curious to witness the other side of Barry's social network and whether his nickname had faded into the past with the rest of their university bad boy days.

Barry was newly engaged to a beautiful office intern with great ambition and the desire to succeed. She was picture perfect with her long flowing blonde hair. Sometimes she looked like she strolled off a photo shoot when prancing into work. Her piercing blue eyes were mesmerizing but not enough to keep the men in the office from staring at her protruding bust line. There were many whispers and gossip going around the office as to how Barry landed such an attractive and young woman. Colleen, who eventually became Barry's wife, brought a few of her girlfriends to the dinner that night. They were as equally attractive as Colleen only single and ready to have a good time. After consuming one too many drinks, Victor ended up at a hotel suite with the more than eager ginger. Unable to remember exactly what happened between them, Victor was sure he committed adultery, or so the pictures on his cell phone proved it. Upon waking the next morning, he was left with little memory of the night before, a huge headache and an empty hotel suite. Victor wondered whether the enthusiastic ginger left him in the suite alone because of a previous scheduled engagement or because she was disappointed in his performance. Either way, Victor didn't want to find out the answer. He always regretted that night and vowed to himself to never speak of it again, to anyone. Victor never knew if Barry and Colleen were ever privy to the happenings of that evening, but neither one of them ever spoke about it. Victor could only assume after all the years passed, the one night stand he participated in but couldn't remember would never be spoken of again in his lifetime.

~16~

Mary extended her arms out to her sides for a long needed stretch like she did most mornings. The bedroom drapes were drawn keeping her suite rather dark. Mary could tell the morning had arrived based on the glow around the outer rim of the curtains. Anticipating a nice long jog for the morning, she pre planned a jogging route through the park adjacent to the hotel. After that, she would come back to the hotel suite to shower and make lunch reservations. She thought about inviting Camden for another lunch filled with food, drink, laughter and storytelling. Although the last story Camden told Mary about was heart wrenching and rather tragic, she was hoping there were a few feel good stories to be told. Listening to him speak about his life helped Mary understand hers a little more. Getting past the abuse and moving on with Victor can't be the whole picture. Is life really all about work and marriage? Why did she always feel so incomplete? How was Richard successful in taking a piece of Mary and leaving her feeling so hollow? Without opening her eyes, she rolled over and felt a warm body next to her. Opening her eyes, she let out a scream.

"What! What! What's wrong?" Camden replied.

"What's wrong is that you are in my bed," she responded.

"We must have fallen asleep last night," Camden offered the most reasonable explanation he could think of.

"Fell asleep, yes that's what probably happened," she agreed. "You don't think we…um…"

"No! I'm pretty sure about that," Camden replied.

"I'm married, this should have never happened," Mary said still thinking more than an innocent sleep over occurred.

"It's okay Mary," Camden assured her. "Nothing happened last night other than two friends forging a lasting friendship."

Mary convinced herself that Camden was telling the truth. After all, they both drank a bit and partook in smoking a joint together; something Mary had only done once before in her life. Mary playfully peeked under the sheets as if to tease Camden but to her surprise, he was stark naked.

"You had a towel on last night. Why do you not have the towel on anymore," Mary asked while increasingly becoming more paranoid again.

Camden started to laugh. Amused by her innocent thinking, he gave the best explanation he could.

"I think you're looking for an excuse to convince yourself, and maybe me, that we had sex last night," he suggested. "Would it have been all that bad?

"No I'm not! I'm merely making a blatant observation," Mary snapped.

"Relax doll. It must have slipped off while I was sleeping. I'm not sure how you sleep on a regular but I have a tendency to move around a lot in my sleep," Camden explained.

"Right, of course," Mary giggled. "I'm not thinking clearly. It's not every day I wake up to find a naked man in my bed, who is not my husband I might add." Mary purposely ignored his questionable attempt at fishing around for sexual relations approval.

"Don't be making this a habit then young lady," Camden teased.

Mary slid out of the bed careful not to expose anymore of what she already had and jetted off into the bathroom. Closing the door behind her, Mary secretly enjoyed Camden's piercing eyes on her backside. It seemed like a lifetime ago when men would gawk at her innocent beauty, only she could never flirt back with the admiring men because Richard would surely offer a few choice remarks. It was always Mary's fault if another man looked at her. Richard's controlling mannerisms and condescending interpretations of the other men's glances would almost always end up in a heated argument. Richard would then go on to raping Mary just to teach her a lesson as to what the glances from other men really meant inside their sick heads.

"They don't look at you like a fine piece of art," Richard would explain. "They are looking at you like a hot piece of ass."

Mary scrubbed herself down in the shower desperately trying to clean off her filthy approval of Camden's bedroom glances. Softly rubbing soap over her stomach, she envisioned what it would be like to have a tiny baby growing inside. She couldn't be certain but she felt like her stomach could be protruding a little more than it normally did. She found herself picturing Camden playing with a young toddler. They would be chasing each other around a big open field with no cares or schedules. She immediately felt immense sorrow for the loss of his unborn child. Putting an immediate halt on her thoughts, she didn't want to explore her already growing connection with a man she hardly knew. How was it that she could allow herself to enjoy the attention of another man? Richard's years of abuse taught her to ignore the glances, whistles and snide comments of other men who passed her. Their ignorant behaviours where merely reflections of the actions they wanted to commit. This was why she loved Victor so much. Victor never treated her with crude or malice actions. He was also very sensitive to her needs. His perfectly balanced gesticulations are what won her love. So why now did Mary remotely enjoy the attention of another man?

Quietly in the other room, Camden remained naked and surprisingly comfortable on her bed waiting for his turn to use the shower. He contemplated joining Mary in the shower but quickly thought better of it. The timing wasn't right yet. He would have his sweet Mary soon enough but he knew he had to play his cards perfectly to win her over. Glancing though his phone, he opened his camera roll to go through the photos he took the night prior. There must have been two dozen pictures of him and Mary all cozy in bed together. Each picture he flipped through put a bigger smile on his face. Camden caressed himself harder and faster with every new picture he viewed. His arousal peaked in perfect timing to the last picture taken of Mary in a very compromising pose. These pictures where the perfect tool to use as either blackmail or evidence but only Camden had the resources to decide the direction of use. Camden wrapped the towel around his waist and walked over to the full length mirror that was conveniently situated on the wall adjacent to the bed. Seemingly happy with his evening's events, Camden offered a smug smile and snapped a few selfie's. He was quite happy with himself and equally pleased that the date rape drug he gave Mary in her wine the night prior was the perfect dose to knock her out. After changing the filter and contrast on the picture he saved the photo that he thought was the best one. Camden posted the picture to his social media site with the caption *paybacks are sexy*.

"One more for the road," Camden blurted out loud to himself.

Camden scanned through some of the risky pictures of Mary that he captured the night before. He was careful to choose an innocent picture of a scantily clad Mary all tucked in to her hotel suite bed. Vigilant not to choose a picture that exposed too much of her delicate skin but just enough skin exposure to show off her sensual and natural beauty.

"Perfect," Camden said through a tight lipped grin. "This ought to show him how peaceful and relaxed his wife is without him," he added.

Camden attached the picture to a short e-mail addressed to Victor, letting him know that she was safe and recovering from a night of drinking. Camden added that things could have been worse but he was diligently working every moment of the day to ensure her safety. He was sure to include that Victor had nothing to worry about, that acting out and poor behaviour was something of a natural progression at the start of therapy. Mary would be re-living some horrific memories and sometimes the patient acted out of anger and guilt. Camden also assured Victor that Mary was in a very safe environment and that he would personally see to it that she stay safe. With those words, Camden hit the send button and shut off his phone.

"You poor bastard," Camden let escape from his mouth just as Mary came out of the bathroom.

"Who's a poor bastard?" Mary asked innocently while towel drying her hair.

"No one in particular per say," Camden replied offering a nervous laugh. "I was commenting on the guy on the street that just lost his hat to the wind. I watched him chase it down the street before he was able to catch up to it.

"That wind has really picked up," Mary noted. "It looks like we are in for some rain today too."

"I need to jump into the shower and get washed up," Camden reported. "I need to step out and get some errands done which will probably take up most of the day, but if you want we can meet up for dinner again tonight?"

"I understand how this works. Daytime escapes and evening delights," Mary joked.

Mary couldn't understand why she was acting so foolish around Camden. Something about him brought out the playful girl in her and she liked it. Although it scared Mary to think that her flirtatious actions were sure to land her in some hard situations, she was that much more confident that she wouldn't cross any lines. The problem with that thinking was that she knew she already crossed a line by allowing him to spend the night with her. Either way, Mary liked how she has been feeling. Somehow she felt more free and liberated than she had ever felt before. Besides, getting away to Toronto was to allow her to find herself and to start her healing process. A way to come back to Victor with a new found sense of who she really was. To let go of her past and forge a new present that was supposed to lead her to a great future. Mary was determined to find solace in her life, at any cost.

~17~

Victor awoke to a panic attack, something he had never experienced before. His excessive sweating left his sheets drenched. He could feel his heart racing and the sharp chest pain he was experiencing was excruciating. The more he tried to get himself out of bed, the harder it was for him to move. He could feel his throat closing leaving him gasping for air. Victor knew that he had been under a tremendous amount of stress so he was fairly confident he would be fine as soon as he could get his breathing under control. His short shallow breaths slowly lengthened offering him more and more oxygen with every breath he fought for. Once he managed to get his breathing under control, Victor sat up in bed and reached for the glass of water on his bedside table. Unable to concentrate on much these days, he picked his cell phone up and called into the office to inform them that he would be taking a short leave of absence. He instructed his secretary to clear his schedule for the day and put a memo out to his colleagues to apologise for his unexpected and abrupt leave of absence. Victor assured his assistant that he was fine but needed to travel to Toronto to take care of a very important business matter. There was nothing more important to Victor than Mary. Although his secretary assumed it had something to do with Mary, she would never intrude on his personal matters by asking. She did as she was instructed and left it at that. Victor could always rely on Cynthia's capable work ethics and abilities. She's been with his firm from its conception and remained loyal throughout his career. Cynthia loved what she did as a career and dedicated her entire life to her work. She never married although she was known to date a few men in her time. She never had the urge to start a family nor wanted a committed relationship. She always thought it complicated life regardless of personal choices, age or financial situation. Time and time again, Cynthia witness the reunion and bitter break ups from all the people close to her. She didn't want to add to the statistic of one more broken marriage. Her beauty and charm was well sought after in her younger days but as time aged her face and body, she became even more thankful to have divulged herself into her work.

"I'll send the itinerary over to you via e-mail as soon as I receive the confirmation booking," Cynthia told Victor.

"Thank you Cynthia and please prepare a hefty bonus for yourself. I will sign off on it and Barry can have Administration release it to you by tomorrow. Please take this gift and pamper yourself however you feel fit. You deserve so much more but please know that I value your loyalty and unwavering dedication to my firm and me," Victor explained.

"Thank you very much. I do appreciate your recognition of my hard work Sir," Cynthia replied with gratitude.

Victor hung up from the call and calmly took a few deep breaths in and slowly exhaled. Recognizing that he needed to slow down a bit, his next phone call was to book a massage to help ease his tension. Ever since his car accident, Victor went to regular massage therapy to help with his non life threatening injuries. He noticed massage therapy helped with his muscle tension so he continued with the therapy even though his Doctor gave him a clean bill of health. Hopefully his massage will coincide nicely with his flight time out to Toronto. Victor's anxiety increased with the thought of his trip to Toronto being in vain. What if Mary completely rejected his visit or worse, had already moved hotels and he couldn't find her. The latter shouldn't be a problem because Camden would know her whereabouts. A flood of emotions started to overcome him and instantly he could feel his heart palpitations start with fluttering and erratically heart beats. Fearful of another anxiety attack, Victor shifted his focus on getting a precious gift for his wife upon his surprise visit. There's just one more phone call he had to squeeze in before he booked his massage and then he would need to get packing for his trip to Toronto.

Victor had been planning a very special and extremely romantic getaway for the two of them to a remote island in Bora Bora for their ten year anniversary. It was meant to be a complete surprise to Mary. Victor had been attentive to her work schedule and pre-arranged a two week open schedule in March with her Assistant already. The final details of planned meals, nightly entertainment and day excursions had yet to be confirmed but everything else had been considered and reserved. Victor arranged one piece of fine hand crafted jewellery for everyday they are away and had his personal jeweller make plans for it to be delivered to the Island ahead of time. Victor even pre arranged to have the jewellery item placed on her bedside with a short pre written love note and a single rose on a regular basis through the hotel's concierge.

The sound of Victor's cell phone notification tone brought him back to the present moment. Remembering that he gave specific instructions to Cynthia to forward his itinerary he snatched up his cell phone eager to review the Toronto booking. With great disappointment, Cynthia apologized that the first direct flight wouldn't be possible until the next morning and that she would hold off in booking until further instructions were given to her. Victor stared at his e-mail for what appeared to be a lifetime. With so many thoughts running through his mind, he couldn't seem to make an educated decision. On one hand, he wanted to rush out to Toronto to ensure Mary was okay. Unable to shake his uneasy feeling about her travels, he wanted to reply back to Cynthia to instruct her to book the flight anyway. On the other hand, Victor also wanted to honour Mary's personal request to give her some space and time to sort through her own issues. Victor paced back and forth while contemplating his decision in his head. Although he knew the right choice was to let Mary deal with things on her own, he had always been the one who helped her get back on her emotional feet. Maybe that was the whole problem. Perhaps all those times he tried to ground her from her emotional chaos, he was in fact only placing a band aid on the real problem. What if the real problem was in fact Mary needing to learn to take charge of her own life including her emotions and past experiences? She always had Victor to cushion her hard realities. Mary never had to steamroll through any of her raw emotions on her own.

Victor noticed that he had an unread e-mail from Camden. He could feel his heart start to race again and hoped it was an update on Mary. He opened the attachment and stared at Mary peacefully asleep in her hotel suite. At that moment, Victor decided to hold off on his trip to Toronto, even though a small voice in his head kept telling him otherwise. Victor physically felt sick to his stomach at the thought that Mary could be in some serious turmoil and he was not there to shelter her from it. Knowing that Camden was there to keep her safe, he diverted his plan from being there in person to requesting Camden in taking a larger role with Mary. He reviewed his text message from Camden, more specifically the comment he made of how Mary drank too much the night before but that it was a natural progression to healing. Victor replied to Camden's message asking him to do whatever he needed to stay close to Mary. Victor offered to double his compensation and requested constant feedback whenever possible. Now Victor waited on Camden's response. Almost expecting a reply immediately, Victor grew concerned when he didn't hear back. It had been nearly five minutes and Victor still had no reply from Camden. Ten minutes passed and still nothing which drove Victor into another anxiety attack. Victor made his way into the bathroom to splash cold water onto his face. He looked at his very pale reflection in the mirror and realized for the first time how much he had aged. His youthful and boyish face had matured into a masculine but chiselled version of his father's. His once luscious and thick dark hair had slowly started thinning. Victor poked at a few stray grey hairs and contemplated pulling them out. He decided against it rather quickly. He knew it was a myth but just the thought of two additional grey hairs growing in replace to the pulled one didn't appeal to him. Aging was a natural progression in life and he was determined to embrace the process. Mary always told him that men with salt and pepper hair colour looked handsome and distinguished. Growing increasingly worried when he didn't hear back from Camden, Victor picked up his cell to place a direct call to him. Just before he pushed the call button, a text message from Camden came through. He responded with a simple "yes boss, no worries."

~18~

Gwen Landucci was always the first one to arrive at the office. Her senior assistant title looked great on her business cards but she knew whole heartedly that she was given that title out of pure guilt. Gwen accepted the generous promotion and pay raise that accompanied it knowing full well her past work experience had not warranted the reward. From that day onward, she vowed to dedicate her free time to advancing her skill set. She was set on showing her dedication and worth to her job and nothing else mattered. Gwen was known to be a very happy person who had an innate ability to light up a room when she walked into it. Life circumstances and failed life dreams changed her mostly positive outlook on life. Her beauty went far beyond her looks. Her innocent face accompanied her soul of merit, a trait that came quite natural to her. Her luscious locks of wavy brown hair sat perfectly on her head without much fuss. She was blessed with pure voluptuous lips that most women paid to have. Although she had a rather delicate frame, her personality could storm through any kind of quagmire. She walks with a leg brace and she's pretty confident arthritis is setting in on her once badly damaged knee but Gwen was never one to quit or give up on something. Gwen was tough with her words but anyone who knew her well enough, knew she was a plain old softy inside.

The October weather was full of high winds and rainy days. That morning was no different than any other stormy fall day. Staring out the office window with her coffee in hand, Gwen recognized her boss immediately from seven floors up. She hadn't witnessed him come into the office for a few weeks but that was nothing out of the ordinary for her. Gwen was a master at manipulating Doctor Copeland's patient schedule. After many years of working for the often flighty doctor, Gwen knew exactly how to keep his patients satisfied with their treatment plans as well as unsuspicious of his non traditional treatment methods. When patients would show up for their therapy session and the unabated Doctor was a no show, Gwen would often supply the patient with a sociotherapy exercise to keep them busy for the week. If the Doctor was absent longer than a week, Gwen was sure to have a part two section for follow up.

Gwen shuffled around at her desk gathering any missed messages and client files that needed updated for when the Doctor arrived. She was never certain on the Doctor's office attendance but what she did know for sure is that he was mostly grumpy. Gwen chalked his less than desired demeanor up to having to listen to everyone else's problems on a regular basis, that and his unfortunate and regrettable past. Gwen's been part of Doctor Copeland's life, long before he turned into a gloomy and melancholy man.

"Good morning Gwen, how is your morning going so far?" the doctor asked with great joy.

"Ummm, ahhmmm," Gwen cleared her throat. "My day has been great so far, Doctor, and you?"

Clearly Gwen was surprised to witness such happiness emanating from the normally quiet and wretched doctor.

"Here are your missed calls and messages since the last time we spoke," she explained.

"Thank you Gwen," he replied while taking the bundle of pink message papers from her hand.

Flipping through the rather big stack of messages, the doctor stopped at one halfway through the pile and beamed the biggest smile Gwen had ever seen him show.

"Here's the client files that have completed their sociotherapy exercises that you will need to read through and offer comments. You don't have any clients booked in today because I wasn't sure of your office schedule," Gwen explained.

"Great job Gwen!" Doctor Copeland exclaimed in a loud and joyful voice. "Have you called any of these new clients back to book introduction appointments yet?"

"No I haven't…" she started to explain.

"Good…good…then I will take care of this myself," he stated.

Gwen felt slightly uneasy with the doctor. His particular behaviour was not something she had ever witnessed. He held a slight grin on his face but the look in his eyes was somewhere between empty and wild. Gwen observed his breakdown years ago which was a very unpleasant experience for them both. She didn't wish to be a spectator to that ever again but she feared he was slowly sliding into the crazy zone again. Gwen contemplated speaking to him about taking a break from work but felt apprehensive about bringing up the subject. Instead she prepared a glass of water with a squeeze of fresh lemon and went to deliver it to his office. Gwen tapped lightly on his office door careful not to rattle the private sign dangling from a small nail that stuck out ever so slightly.

"Come in," Doctor Copeland responded.

Gwen entered his private office and client room slowly careful not to spill his water. Shaking slightly from her leg brace but mostly because she knew she was about to step on some pretty thin ice with what she was about to ask him.

"I brought you some fresh lemon water," Gwen started off with.

"Thank you Gwen. Leave it on my desk please," he replied still staring at the pink message slip that caught his eye moments before at her desk.

Gwen reached over to place the water on his desk. As she reached over to set the glass down, she caught a glimpse at the message that seemed to be mesmerizing him. It was a message left by a woman named Mary, one of the newest messages.

"I don't mean to intrude Doctor, but I do remember that patient's call should you need further details," Gwen offered.

"You do?" Doctor Copeland said as he cleared his throat and sat up erect in his chair.

"Yes I do. Obviously she stated that her name was Mary and gave her contact number but she sounded slightly nervous. Also, she did say that she was not from this area but was visiting for a short while," Gwen reported.

"Oh, really? Did she happen to mention how long her short visit actually was?" he inquired.

"No she didn't unfortunately. I didn't make an introduction appointment with her either because I wasn't sure if you were accepting out of town patients yet," Gwen explained.

"Yes, but of course you wouldn't know that. Good work Gwen and thank you. That is all for now," the Doctor concluded.

Without noticing Gwen still standing in front of his desk, Doctor Copeland sipped on his water and then started to mumble to himself all while slightly salivating.

"Are you okay Doctor? Can I get you anything else?" Gwen said still observing his odd behaviour.

"I'm fine!" he shouted. "I thought I excused you already?"

"You did Doctor Copeland but please know this is difficult for me to say," Gwen started.

"Gwen! We've been friends for a very long time so please, if there is something you need to say then just say it already," he retorted.

"Okay, well, it's just…" Gwen tried to find the right words.

"Okay Gwen, please take a seat and try to start over with a clear train of thought. Oh, and please stop addressing me so formally when there are no patients around," he ordered with a stern tone.

"Sorry, it's a habit, Camden. We have been friends for a very long time. I'm not just someone who works for you. I'm your friend. I've been your friend since you met your late wife. Hell, I was your wife's best friend. I know how difficult it's been for you to lose her and your baby. I hate to drudge up the past but I know you pretty well and I can tell that something is off with you. Something is just not right but I can't quite put my finger on it. You're not back into the drugs again are you?" she asked with hesitation.

"God no! Well I did smoke a little pot the other night but I assure you it was just to mellow out a bit. I promise you that I am fine. In fact, I haven't felt this good for a very long time.

"Okay if that's your explanation then I will have to accept it," Gwen said.

"It's not my explanation as you put it. It's the truth of the matter and I'm sorry you can't be content with the fact that I'm finally moving past that horrible time in my life. Onward and upward is my new motto," Camden stated.

"If you say so Boss, but be sure to know that you mean a lot to me. You're not just my boss, you're also my friend," she told him. "My best friend."

"Gwen," Camden softly said. "You know you're so much more than just my friend."

And with those words, Gwen's face lit up light a glowing Christmas tree. Gwen had always loved Camden only she could never tell him because he was the husband to her then best friend. She adored his law school charm but when he fell in love with Adrianna she professed to never let her true feelings show. Gwen stood as maid of honour to Adrianna but secretly wished it was her walking down the aisle with Camden and not her best friend. In some wild fantasy; after the tragic death of Adrianna, Gwen hoped Camden would need her more than ever and turn to her for the comfort and support a grieving husband would need. Instead, Camden turned to drugs and depression. Regardless of the path Camden had headed down, Gwen vowed to stay close and loyal to her one true love and there was nothing she wouldn't do for him.

~19~

Excited for her dinner plans, Mary shopped for the perfect dinner outfit. She was careful not to choose anything too revealing but wanted the perfect scantily clad piece to leave just enough room for imagination. She found a high-lo black lace gown that accented her perfectly long lean legs. Mary finished the outfit with a red heal to add a pop of colour. It's alluring shade screamed power and confidence; red was known to be the colour of seduction. Mary loved wearing red, not that she needed the extra attention but she felt extra sexy when she wore the lovable colour. The love shade gave an extra boost to her black dress, not that her almost transparent dress needed a boost. Why she was trying to appear sexy to other men was unknown to her. All she knew was that she liked the way she felt around Camden and somehow his presence helped her feel alive and whole again.

When Mary snapped back into reality, she heard her cell phone ring. She was eager to take the call; knowing only one person had her number.

"Hello?" Mary softly answered.

"How's your day going Beautiful?" Camden asked.

"It's been fantastic so far. I bought a new dress for tonight's dinner," she proclaimed with glee.

"Tonight's dinner?" he questioned.

"Ah yeah, I thought we made dinner plans this morning before you left?" Mary inquired. "Did something come up?"

"No no, nothing has come up. I'm just fooling with you. I've already made reservations to a nice restaurant around your hotel area. I've had dinner there a few times and absolutely love everything on their menu," Camden said sounding proud.

"Are you going to leave me in suspense or will you tell me where we are going ahead of time?" Mary playfully asked.

"Well now that I know you are so interested in the venue, I think I'll leave you guessing," he said.

"Somewhere in my area that you've frequented," Mary quizzed. "How close to my hotel?"

"Inquiring minds do want to know! I'll give you a hint. It's in the financial district," he mentioned.

"There must be over two hundred restaurants in the financial district. Can you narrow the guessing game down slightly?" Mary asked.

"Okay, here is the most subtle hint I can possibly give you. The owner of the restaurant is Mark McEwan.

"Oh yes I know," Mary spewed like a small school girl. It's Bymark isn't it?"

"You guessed that pretty quickly," Camden said while laughing. "Did the owners name give it away that easily?"

"I'm actually a big fan of his group of restaurants and besides, who hasn't wanted to eat at one of his restaurant after witnessing him being a judge on Top Chef Canada?" she bantered. "Tell me though, how are you able to afford all of this on a cab drivers salary? I'm sorry was that too personal?"

"Alright there Grasshopper, settle down a bit would you? One question at a time," Camden spoke taking control of the conversation again. "I never guessed you to be the star struck kind of girl but then again, we are just getting to know each other better. How I can afford fine dining is a personal question but lucky for you I'm a fairly transparent guy. The short answer is that I know how to save and manage my money and besides, I think you seem to forget that Toronto is not as expensive to live in as New York City. Don't over think things Pretty Lady because there are a few more surprises in store for you."

"By the way, I'm not star struck but you have caught my attention again. I love surprises," Mary stated. "So spill it because the anticipation is killing me."

"Well surprise number one is that our menu for the evening has already been arranged so there will be no need to fuss over the menu items. Surprise number two is that I heard through the grapevine that some Hollywood celebrities are known to dine there on occasion; you know for us non star struck kind of people that we are. Although they are being tight lipped about who will be there tonight, I'm pretty positive it will be a celebrity of higher status.

"That sounds great," Mary chimed in. "Let me be clear to you that I've never been star struck so the celebrity thing doesn't excite me too much but I appreciate the try."

"The try?" Camden repeated. "No honey, this isn't just a try. I have so much already planned it's going to make your pretty little head spin."

"Wow okay then," she blurted out. "I hope you didn't go out of your way or anything. You know it's just dinner between two new friends."

"Yes, of course. I'm only joking around with you," he said trying to sound calm and collected. "No mariachi band then?"

"You're such a joker sometimes," Mary laughed.

Looking at her watch, Mary realized that half the day had gone to shopping already.

"There's still so much I need to get done today so I'm going to let you go so I can try and complete today's agenda," Mary declared.

"What else could a perfectly balanced but delicate beautiful flower like you possibly need to get done today?" he asked.

"Oh there is plenty to do and seeing as the personal driver I had set up for the day was unavailable, I've had to wait for taxi's most of the day," she jabbed.

"I'm sorry for that, truly I am," he apologized not because he was sorry for her inconvenience but because he had to part from her presence for most of the day. "Do you want me to arrange for someone else to come and drive for you today?"

"Oh my goodness no but thank you. That's not what I meant when I said that. I just meant that waiting for random cabs was eating up some of my time when I could be getting other things done," she tried to explain.

"Well perhaps I could have my assistant Gwen take care of some things on your behalf. That would free up your time to get whatever it is you need to get done," Camden uttered.

"That's a very generous offer and I think I will take you up on the offer," she accepted.

"Okay now we're getting somewhere," he proclaimed. "I can call her now to start her on your list of things to be done. What will it be?"

"I already placed a call to a therapist that I wanted to go see while I'm in town for a bit. Without getting into too much detail, there are a few things in my past that I would like to try and work through so I thought speaking to a therapist could assist me with that," Mary explained.

"I'm not sure my assistant can speak to your therapist for you," he probed.

"No silly! I don't want your assistant speaking to the therapist. I need her, uummm Gwen, to call him for me to book an appointment," Mary expressed.

"So you've called already but you need my assistant to call again?" Camden reiterated. "Did you miss the first appointment?"

"No I never even had an appointment. That's the problem. I called and left a message but no one has returned my call. I find it strange that a professional office wouldn't return a potentially new client's telephone call," Mary expelled with concern in her voice.

"That is strange," Camden added for a realistic but dramatic effect.

"So do you think your assistant could call Doctor Copeland's office to set up an appointment on my behalf?" she asked.

Without letting out too much excitement, Camden replied "Absolutely! Consider it done already," He was grinning so big his cheeks started to hurt.

"Thank you a tonne. Could you please have Gwen call me directly to confirm the appointment date? Make sure you give her my new number too?" Mary ordered.

"That's it!" Camden declared. "Mystery solved."

"What mystery? Are we solving mysteries now?" Mary inquired. "I don't have time for mysteries."

"The mystery as to why you haven't heard back from this Doctor Copeland yet," he announced sounding rather proud. Proud that he didn't have to try and come up with some excuse as to why he hadn't returned her call yet and proud that everything was falling perfectly into place.

"I must be tired or have completely lost my mind because I'm not catching on to the solved mystery," Mary admitted.

"Doctor Copeland's office hasn't called you back because you changed your cell phone number," he accurately stated.

"Yes but of course. That explains it. It is beyond me why I didn't think of that myself," Mary admitted feeling foolish. "Clearly my mind has wondered into the no thinking zone again. See, this is exactly why I need to see a therapist. Hopefully this doctor can help me screw my head on straight."

"I'm glad that's settled," he said all while beaming full of joy. Camden had been racking his brain to find an excuse he could use as to why he never returned her initial call for an appointment but now he didn't need an excuse. One practically fell at his feet. He took it as a sign that everything was happening as it should be which gave him an idea. He knew how he was going to keep his real identity secret from Mary. His genius idea would allow him to continue being her friend and her therapist without her even having the slightest clue.

"Okay Mary my other line is ringing through so I'll pick you up at six," Camden stated and ended the call without waiting for her response.

Mary just looked at her phone slightly surprised with his prompt call dismissal. There were a few more things on her list of to do's that she could have delegated to his assistant and contemplated calling Camden back to have his assistant complete them too.

~20~

Camden started the evening celebration early with a glass of wine and light music. Prancing around his apartment, he could still feel the resonating glee of his earlier conversation with Mary. Camden was eager to get his evening started but first he had to place a call to Gwen to ensure his instructions to her were clear. Dialing Gwen's personal cell number was something Camden has done thousands of times prior so it was no wonder that he had the number memorized.

Gwen answered after the second ring. "Hi Camden what's up?"

"Hello there Gwenevere," he playfully said.

"Gwenevere here at your service my Lord," letting out a laugh, Gwen decided to play along. After all he was her secret true love and she longed for any bit of attention he gave her.

When she was in his company, she acted like a foolish little girl with a crush. How Camden hadn't caught on to her weird and quirky behaviour while she was around him was beyond her. Maybe he just thought she was strange and odd all the time. Maybe he just didn't care enough to even give her behaviour a second thought, or maybe he was so wrapped up in his own personal grief he hadn't even allowed himself to explore the option of having a relationship with another woman.

"Did you get all that?" Camden asked snapping Gwen out of her self-indulging daydream.

"I was dreaming! I was daydreaming to be exact. As embarrassed as I am to admit this, I didn't hear one single word you said," she confessed.

"Okay I get it, its fine. Come to my apartment now. There are a few important issues that I need to address with you," he instructed her.

Not having any kind of life, Gwen was always able to succumb to all of Camden's demands. She only wished his demands where of a passionate type rather than work.

"I'm on my way," Gwen replied in a monotone voice.

"Great and thank you," he said. "Oh and Gwen, wear something nice."

Gwen was a little shocked with his last comment. "What did he mean by wear something nice?" she thought out loud. Camden never requested anything of a personal matter from her before.

"He has either lost his mind or it's my lucky day," she said to herself.

Gwen riffled through her closet and came across a new outfit she bought a short while ago but never got the chance to wear it anywhere. The simple but elegant black dress could be used for multiple occasions either dressed up or casual. Seeing as Camden didn't offer any details on what sort of "nice" he had in mind, Gwen thought it would be best to pair the tight black dress with a nude wrap. This gave the dress a not so formal look if needed. She could easily remove the wrap to bring formality back to the outfit should it be required. The dress fell below her knee giving her availability to wear her knee brace without much visibility from others. Without the brace, her knee was unstable and she didn't want to risk falling especially when she was pairing her dress with gorgeous Anne Michelle studded t-strap pumps. Gwen always felt better about herself when she dressed up in nice clothes. Her militant posture and stroke of confidence proved to be her secret advantage when it came to Camden.

"Holy smokes Woman you look amazing," Camden said as he opened the door to his apartment upon her arrival.

"Thank you Camden. I don't think you've ever really offered me such a wonderful compliment before. In fact, I don't think you've ever really noticed much of me outside of work," Gwen added.

"That's not true at all Gwen. You are a very attractive woman but you work for me so it would be very unprofessional of me to gawk or say inappropriate comments while in the office," he confessed.

"Well it's a good thing we're not at the office then," Gwen teased.

"Please come in," Camden gestured. "Where are my manners leaving you standing in the hallway?"

"Oh don't be so hard on yourself," she joked. "I have that effect on men."

"You definitely have something on me," he admitted. "But I'm thinking more of a spell because I can't stop staring at you."

Gwen smiled to herself and internally she could feel the butterflies going wild around in her stomach. She had waited many years to hear those exact words come out of Camden's mouth. Gwen was pretty sure Adrianna would offer her blessing if she and Camden ever became a couple.

"Would you care for a glass of wine?" Camden asked. "Loosen you up a bit, you seem rather tense."

"Yes please," Gwen answered. "I wouldn't describe it as tense but I am rather nervous."

"What is there to be nervous about? We are two adults having a simple business meeting outside of our work environment that is all," he assured her hoping to put her nervous feelings aside.

"Yes of course but why did you ask me to dress nice," she inquired.

"I asked you to dress nice because we are having pre dinner drinks at Bymark," he explained.

"You're taking me to Bymark for dinner and drinks?" Gwen asked.

"Drinks yes, dinner no," he responded quickly.

"Okay I give up," Gwen said throwing her hands up into the air.

"Please let me explain in simple terms," he said rather disgruntled.

"Okay first off, there is no need to speak to me in that manner and secondly, I'm not a mind reader so a simple explanation is generally what happens when two people are trying to converse with one another," she conveyed.

"How did this just turn ugly?" Camden questioned.

"I'm not trying to make anything ugly, I seriously just need to know what you're talking about," Gwen tried to explain in a softer tone.

"We are going to go to Bymark to have some drinks and discuss a few office matters. Then I will be having dinner with a woman named Mary," Camden began to explain as simple as he could.

"I get it now. I'm nearly a buffer to loosen you up for your big dinner date with Mary. Is that the same Mary that left you a message at the office that had you smiling from here to the moon and back?" Gwen said clearly crossing the professional line.

"What has gotten into you lately? First you question me at the office and now you're throwing around attitude like its on sale," Camden snapped back.

"I'm sorry. I'm so sorry, you're right. I have no idea why I'm acting like this lately. Please forgive my rude behaviour," she uttered.

Gwen knew exactly why she was acting the way she was. Her overzealous feelings for the fine looking doctor had taken over her professional relationship with him. The reality of her only being called to his apartment for a business meeting crushed her high hopes of finally getting the man of her dreams into her world.

"Let's get back to when I first opened the door and I saw this beautiful breath of fresh air standing in front of me, Camden said trying to make the conversation positive again.

The last thing he wanted or needed at the moment was for Gwen to turn her back on him, especially now when he needed her the most; to help execute his well thought out plan.

"So just drinks it is," Gwen agreed.

"Yes my dear and speaking of drinks, we need to head out now before it gets too late," Camden ordered.

The taxi ride to the restaurant was fairly quick considering the Friday traffic. They settled into the restaurant with a glass of red wine to welcome their early arrival. Their table was situated in a quiet area of the restaurant nestled between an exposed brick wall and a few smaller tables. Privacy was a key instruction when Camden booked the reservations. He wanted to ensure privacy for his new client and even more privacy for the woman who was occupying most of his days lately. Camden wasn't one hundred percent sure how the evening was going to play out but one thing he was certain of was that he needed to report back to Victor on her progress. He could tell Victor was getting antsy about Mary's well being and needed constant reassurance that she was fine. Camden wanted to make sure Victor's worries were put to ease because he didn't want or need him to show up unexpected. Everything was going to plan and soon enough revenge would be his for the taking.

After some brief small talk, Camden ordered a few more glasses of wine.

"Cheers to you," Camden said trying to start the awkward conversation.

"Cheers to you too," Gwen replied.

Sipping on their wine, Camden reached out and placed his hand on Gwen's. Camden was excellent at reading people and their reactions. That was one of the reasons why Camden was awarded best therapist in Toronto three years in a row. His innate ability to focus on patient weakness to help them overcome personal obstacles was his specialty. Most of the time Camden knew the root of his patient's problems before the patient was even remotely close to even knowing they had a problem. Although the people reading trait was a great tool to have for his profession, Camden often misused his gift to get what he personally wanted.

"So I'm just going to cut to the chase here Gwen," Camden blurted out. "I've invited Mary here to have dinner with me but not as a new client. The truth of the matter is that I have already met Mary before I even knew she called my office to book an appointment with me. With that being said, Mary doesn't know that I am Doctor Camden Copeland either. She hasn't pieced it together because she hasn't actually come into my office and met with me. This is where it gets a little tricky," he tried to explain. "You with me still?"

"Yes I'm following along just fine," Gwen shared sounding annoyed.

"So Mary became my friend first and now she wants to book therapy sessions with me but only she doesn't know I'm the therapist she's been trying to book with. Without getting into all the fine details of how this has all transpired, I told her you are my assistant and that you were going to make the arrangements with the therapist on her behalf. Are you still with me? Camden asked again.

"Yes I am," Gwen replied while nodding her head up and down. "But how am I booking an appointment with you for her when you don't want her to know who you really are? Better yet, why is it exactly that you are hiding your true identity from her?

"Those are some really great questions and I promise you will have all the answers to them in good time, but first I need you to work your magic by providing me with some blank sociotherapy exercises.

"Not a problem at all," Gwen told the doctor all while pulling out her cell phone. With the push of a few buttons she informed him that she sent the templates directly to his personal e-mail account.

"Efficiency has always been one of your best qualities," he let her know her while flashing a smirk.

"So how are you planning to get these exercises to her without her knowing who you are?" Gwen innocently asked.

"Another great question My Dear," Camden revealed making her blush. "I will print them out and give them to her personally but not without first notifying her that you, as my assistant, have set up an introduction meeting."

"Okay, I have to admit that I'm lost now," Gwen confessed.

"Mary already knows that I have an assistant named Gwen. I've already told her that my assistant will set up an appointment on her behalf so now all that's left is for me to tell Mary that the appointment is set up for tomorrow and voila! Mission accomplished," Camden explained with a rather proud smile plastered on his face.

Although Gwen found Camden rather charming and trusted him completely, she couldn't help wonder what more he had up his sleeve. She just had this eerie feeling that there was more to his story.

"So how are you going to get around her not seeing you when you are in a therapy session with her?" she asked still puzzled.

"Simple! I'm going to let her know that you've managed to arrange for some rather unconventional sessions that will strictly take place over the phone," Camden explained. "Phone therapy is the wave of the future and seeing as she is only in town for a short while, Mary can continue with her sessions while she's back in New York.

"New York? Is that where she is from? She didn't mention that in her phone message," Gwen questioned.

"Yes she's from New York but Toronto originally. I've learned quite a bit from her in the past few days of knowing her," Camden lied. He was already quite familiar with all the personal aspects of her life thanks to Victor.

He could see the sadness in Gwen's eyes when he looked at her. Camden knew she would be very disappointed in him if she knew the real reason he was taking an interest in Mary. Camden had always known that Gwen crushed on him but he never felt the connection back. To ensure his plan with Mary went without any hiccups, Camden knew he had to use Gwen as a safety net.

"There will be no need to get into great detail about the phone therapy directly with Mary. All she needs to know is that there's no need to come into the office. All her therapy can and will be done via telephone. I will ensure she gets the details of voice therapy. If she happens to call into the office, please use the utmost professional approach with her. Due to doctor and patient confidentiality, I cannot tell you much more," he smiled.

"I understand Doctor Copeland," Gwen replied.

"Please Gwen. We are on our first official date so call me Camden when out of the office," he said shinning a big boyish white toothed smile.

"A date? I thought you told me that this was strictly a business meeting outside of the office? Gwen tried to clarify.

"It is a meeting and well sort of a date too. You agreed to meet me for drinks outside of the office even though we needed to talk business but I rather enjoy your company and so I declare this a date," he lied again grasping at her heart strings.

In order to have Gwen believe his tiny fib of many more lies to come, Camden leaned into Gwen and gave her a small but gentle kiss.

"This night just went from one to a thousand real quick," she joked still blushing from the unexpected act of affection.

"Okay Mary's just arrived so do me a favour and get back to the office to make up a proper treatment schedule for her to start. E-mail me the attachments and schedule as soon as you have it done. Oh, and remember what I told you about her treatment method. I'll be in touch," he ordered.

With those few words, Gwen was off and running like a good little soldier.

~21~

Victor's concentration levels were next to zero these days. The only thing he could think of was Mary. His unsettling feeling that she was in danger had not dulled. The disconcerted feeling increased in its severity every day that passed. Victor was certain that he had to travel to Toronto to check on her; even if it meant watching her from a close distance. He needed to see with his own eyes that she was okay. His overactive imagination had him putting Mary in some unusual situations and worse yet imagining some horrible events happening to her beyond belief. Knowing what had happened to Mary in her past had not helped to keep his thoughts of her well being in check. There had been nothing to keep his imagination from wondering about what kind of scenario she might have gotten into. Victor thought his leave of absence from work would help calm his fears, allowing him to concentrate on his own health but his lack of workload only added to his over thinking. The worst part was that he had no communication with Mary which amplified his fears. Victor never wanted to overstep his perimeters seeing as Mary herself had demanded space but sometimes relying solely on Camden to report back on her every move didn't offer much relief to his growing concern. After all, what did he really know about Camden since their university days? How well had Camden done with his current career?

"Perhaps I should have looked into him a little more before hiring him to watch over Mary," he said to his reflection in the mirror.

Walking over to his agenda, Victor made a note to research Camden's past. While doing this, Victor took notice to an e-mail from Camden sitting in his inbox. He could feel his anxiety resonating through him, for it was always bittersweet to receive communication from Camden. On one hand Victor got the information he requested on Mary's safety. Her whereabouts and details of her day were usually noted which offered a short burst of relief. On the other hand Victor always emotionally collapsed knowing he was not with her, sharing in her experiences.

Camden's e-mail started with a simple greeting and a quick apology for not reporting on Mary more frequently. He went on to tell Victor that Mary was progressing rather nicely without him by her side and adjusting to her Toronto atmosphere seamlessly. Given their short time together, Camden felt that Mary was almost ready to be more open about her troubles. He was sure she was ready to have an open dialogue about her troubling past. Camden continued to explain how he was winning her friendship more and more and gaining her trust as he was hired to do. Camden openly admitted that Mary was undeniably every bit of woman Victor portrayed her to be. He also wrote that he was proud to know her and that he understood completely why Victor felt the need to keep her safe with all his protective tactics in place. Camden concluded his e-mail by saying they would be having dinner together that evening and that he was confident more progress would organically culminate after an evening of relaxed conversation.

Victor wasn't sure how the e-mail communication was supposed to leave him feeling. Coming from the good doctor, he supposed it was an e-mail meant to comfort his unsettled thoughts about Mary being away however something about the e-mail just didn't sit right with him. It was almost as if Camden's words were smug in nature and somewhat taunting. He read through the e-mail, each time trying to find a hidden message he might have missed buried between the lines. After a few reviews and some daunting speculation, Victor felt his heart slowly breaking, releasing a recrudescence of yearning for Mary and what they once shared. He couldn't understand why Mary was able to open herself up to a stranger but never to him; her husband. Victor had to concentrate on the positives of her trip. After all was said and done, Victor was certain Mary's trip to seek a healed past would offer a new life. Not just a new life to Mary, but also a new life to their marriage, to them both. Without an attempt at therapy, Victor was sure their marriage would never survive; that single thought tore him apart. Mary had always been his dream wife. Whenever Victor thought of settling down to start a family, he pictured doing it with a woman just like Mary. She was nothing short of kind, giving, successful and always putting other's needs ahead of her own. Those were just some of her best qualities. Her one small character downfall was that broken piece within her soul he could never mend. Victor thought her abused heart would restore with the love and nurturing he offered and she deserved but it never did; not yet anyway and Victor held out hope.

Victor decided a quick reply back to Camden's e-mail was necessary so he started by typing a thank you reply and added a quick statement for Camden to make use of their dinner time together. Victor methodically ended his e-mail with a sharp reminder to Camden that he was to continue supplying him with detailed updates in order to stay abreast of Mary's progress.

After hitting send, Victor contemplated retracting the e-mail and adding one more inclusion to keep sending updated text messages with pictures. Victor was convinced seeing pictures of his beautiful wife kept his own worry and anxiety at bay, but it wasn't about him right now. Knowing that Mary was well and out of trouble was about the only thing keeping him off the next flight out to Toronto to check on her well-being. Nothing else mattered to Victor. In fact after sending the e-mail, Victor felt a little foolish about doubting Camden. Erasing his initial agenda note to have Camden's background looked into was an attempt to prove to himself that he was able to trust Camden's professional work. It seemed rather foolish to have his hired personal private investigator investigated. What would come next? His private investigator's investigator investigated? Victor laughed out loud at the thought of it and let his imagination run wild on that lone thought. He pictured an entire city block of black sedans with tinted windows lined up around Mary's hotel with each investigator tailing one another and no one even paying any regard to Mary.

With nothing else to occupy his day, Victor obsessed over Mary's every move. He knew she would be having dinner with Camden that evening, which made Victor watch the time closely. He forgot to ask Camden what time they planned to dine so he shot him another quick e-mail to ask. Much to his surprise, Camden responded immediately informing him that he had some business to take care of first so he would be sending a car service to pick Mary up at her hotel by six o'clock. Camden also told Victor that he was already at the restaurant awaiting her arrival and attached a quirky selfie picture of himself in the lounge at the restaurant.

Victor glanced at his watch anticipating the next half hour to pass incredibly slowly. Hoping he could pass the time quicker, Victor looked into a chartered helicopter company just in case he needed to get to Toronto. This time he wouldn't involve his personal secretary Cynthia, after all he did arrange to take a personal leave of absence. Besides, he was sure she would be off relaxing somewhere with her hefty bonus. Cynthia wasn't known to take a break for herself. Knowing this, Victor thought he should deal with this matter on his own. It didn't take long to locate a company with their headquarters located at the downtown Wall Street heliport in Manhattan. This company promised it could get you anywhere quickly and comfortably. A perfect solution to a not so perfect situation Victor thought.

Victor's anxiety went from top of the heap to zero in a click of the computer mouse. Why didn't he think of this earlier? He sat back in his chair embracing his deflating anxiety as he contacted the chartered company and retained all the information necessary to book his chartered flight to Toronto. He kept a copy of their protocol for the helicopter usage and had it send directly to his personal e-mail. Being a high profile lawyer in the city proved to be valuable in this type of situation. The aviation manager assured Victor that they would dedicate one of their helicopters for his use at anytime over the next couple of weeks. This type of preferred treatment never came cheap. On top of the very large deposit required to reserve such a request, Victor also arranged for a bulky donation to be given to their annual Gala in support of safe aviation. Victor was glad to contribute knowing the benefits to him outweighed the cost.

Victor wore a huge grin proudly as he glanced at the time. Smiling was not something he had been accustomed to in recent days. Now eager to hear back from Camden, he sat patiently and more relaxed since Mary's departure.

~22~

When she walked into the lounge, Camden could physically feel his legs quivering. He was almost sure to fall when he stood up but his unwavering grip on the bar top kept his legs from giving out. Camden wasn't sure if it was Mary's pure beauty that had his wavering legs giving out on him or if it was the fact that he knew what his evening's intentions consisted of. Camden knew all along that he was mastering his end objective solely to create ill intentions; something he was unfamiliar with but planned nonetheless. Arianna would want justice just as he promised her that dreadful night she lay dead in the hospital room. Unable to say good-bye, Camden vowed to seek revenge on the person responsible for taking his true love from him. The evening of the accident was the worst night of his life. The constant heartache that never seemed to go away like Gwen said it would. The love he shared with her could never be erased from his mind. Someone had to be held accountable. As much as he adored Mary, he was sure her pain would be nothing compared to the pain he felt when he lost his wife.

"Hello," Mary greeted with a joyful red lipped smile.

"Hello back. I'm so glad you could make it," Camden offered in return.

"I was surprised to have a car service pick me up and bring me here but I am pleased nonetheless," she told him.

"Was the car up to your standards?" he asked.

"My standards?" Mary laughed. "Do you get the impression that I ride around in stretch limousines back home?"

"Is that what they sent you?" Camden laughed back.

"Yes, but really it's all very good," Mary assured him.

"Phew that's good to know. Next time I'll clearly state that you request a Honda Civic preferably one that is full of rust and squeaks loudly when the brakes are applied," he joked. "Our table is ready just over there."

Camden extended his arm out as if to guide her in the proper direction to their table without directly pointing to it. Mary could see a bouquet of fresh seasonal flowers flawlessly placed in the centre of the table. The soft glowing candles added elegance to the arrangement as well as helped emit the floral scent around the dining area. As they reach the table, Camden pulled Mary's chair out offering nothing more than pure manners as any gentleman would.

"I've arranged for the chef to prepare a special taste menu for us so we shall have no interruptions this evening," Camden declared.

"That is very thoughtful and lovely of you," she said unsure as to why they would need an interruption free evening.

"Before we get on with our night, can we have a quick photo together? It's not very often I'm in the company of such great beauty," Camden said in his first attempt to loosen her up.

"Absolutely," she agreed offering a smile to accompany her blushing cheeks.

"Might I add that you look absolutely radiant tonight? Truthfully, you nearly had me on my knees at the lounge bar when you walked in," Camden admitted omitting his secondary thought.

He waved the waitress over and asked them to take their picture. Camden carefully posed himself close enough to Mary to have it appear they are a couple but casual enough to not provoke any wrongful accusations. He wanted the picture to be perfect before he sent a copy to Victor. Camden wanted to capture Mary's glow, proof she was happy and out of harm's way.

They both reviewed the multiple pictures the waitress took and settle on the one they both agreed was the best. Camden quickly offered to send a copy to Mary in which she gracefully accepted. Keeping his cell phone close to his body, Camden sent the picture to Victor with a quick caption indicating all was good. Then with the push of a few more buttons he sent another copy to Mary.

"Tonight we are here to celebrate you," Camden declared.

"Me? Why me?" Mary asked.

"Because you are you," he added not sure where to go with that question.

"Okay, we will celebrate me but not until we celebrate you too," she stated.

"To us!" Camden said picking up his glass of Prosecco.

"To us," Mary agreed. "This champagne is nice."

"Why thank you Mary. I chose a Prosecco made in Italy specifically because I prefer a lighter sprit wine and it compliments the taster menu the chef has custom made for our visit tonight," Camden explained trying to sound knowledgeable about wines.

"Wow, okay it sounds like you have had this evening planned out for a while now," she innocently stated.

"No, no planning involved," he quickly retorted.

"I didn't mean to offend you," Mary said sensing his instant tension.

"Oh I'm not offended," he offered. "I just think it's important to know that I just planned this evening spur of the moment. Truthfully I eat here all the time and well, they kind of know me here."

"I feel so silly that I said that in the first place, really I didn't mean it the way it came out," Mary said apologetically.

"Don't worry about it, really. So how was your day?" Camden asked quickly changing the subject.

"My day was great. On top of anticipating tonight's dinner, I finally made an appointment with a psychologist I've wanted to see since I arrived here," she offered.

"A psychologist? Camden said acting surprised.

"Yes," she said feeling a little vulnerable. Mary was not one to open up to anyone let alone someone she just met. "Truthfully I'm guilty of letting my past get in the way of my day to day functioning."

"That's nothing to be ashamed of. Many people in society let their behaviours get in the way of their everyday life. I'm even guilty of it on occasion, Camden said trying to be empathetic toward her. "I'm impressed you've reached out to speak to a professional about it. Most people wouldn't."

"I've struggled with some unruly demons during some rather unattractive events from my past," she told him hoping to clear the confusion.

Camden could feel his excitement building internally. He had waited for this culminating moment for quite some time now. His visualizations on how it would take place were not exactly how he imagined them to be but nonetheless, his revelations were coming to life. Knowing that there was still much more work ahead of him, he methodically poured more wine into Mary's glass hoping the effects of the alcohol would help loosen her up.

"So tell me a little about this psychologist you've found," he asked hoping to sound engaged.

"I don't know too much about him but sometimes I think the less you know the better," Mary admitted.

"I'm not sure if I agree with that statement Mary, but as long as you're comfortable with him or her then your therapy should be just as you intend it to be," he offered. "When is your first meeting?"

"Well that is an interesting question," Mary stated.

"I'm not sure why it's so interesting but I have a sneaking suspicion you are about to tell me why," he joked hoping to lighten the mood as well as ease her transition into giving him more information.

"Not that I have a whole lot of experience in seeking a professional ear from a psychologist but I was under the assumption that I would be making an appointment to go into his office and speak with him one on one," Mary tried to clarify. "You know, like they do in the movies."

"So what is your appointment for if not to meet in his office?" Camden asked. "He's not one of these creeps that want to meet you in some unexpected tavern for drinks or something is he?"

"No, it's nothing like that," Mary smiled secretly soaking in Camden's concern.

"Well you're smiling so it can't be all that bad," he added.

"No, it's not bad at all. Maybe I've watched too many movies but I just always thought therapy sessions happened in a small office with a big comfortable lounge chair with a therapist sitting across from you as you babble your sorrows away," she confessed.

"So if you're not meeting in his office, then where are you planning to meet with him," he questioned further.

"Well that just it. I'm not meeting with him at all," Mary tried to explain.

"Okay, now you have me really confused. You scheduled a meeting with this psychologist but you're not meeting with him? Camden sounded genuine with his probing questions and concerns.

"I'm sorry for sounding so confusing. Apparently there is some new methodology that this therapist uses for clients that travel or who don't live locally to his office," Mary further explained, hoping to enlighten Camden.

"It sounds interesting. Care to tell me what this new therapy tactic consists of?" he asked trying hard to sound intrigued.

"Because you sound so invested in my therapy choice, I will be seeking treatment verbally over the telephone," Mary finally exposed her intentions. "Is that weird?"

At this point of the conversation, Camden knew he was getting deeper into Mary's head. He was winning her trust with every moment that passed and with every glass of Prosecco poured. The mere fact that she was opening up to him about her therapy was a small miracle in itself let alone asking him for his unsolicited advice.

"No, it's not weird at all. I'm fairly certain that this is the wave of the future. Most people lead a painfully busy lifestyle and making time for office therapy is not something most of us are willing to do or even can do for that matter. Besides, there are so many different forms of communication these days. Therapist would need to tap into some of those avenues to keep their practice alive and growing," he divulged in hopes his explanation satisfied her lingering doubt.

"You make it all sound so logical," she admitted. "Are you sure you're not a secret psychologist?

Turning a pale shade of pink, Camden shuffled uncomfortably in his seat.

"I'm flattered you think so highly of me," he effortlessly covered.

"You're just so easy to speak to. Opening up to you seems to come so natural to me. I hope my therapist is just as easy going as you are," she admitted. "I'm somewhat anxious to even speak to him over the phone."

"Don't be silly, you'll be just fine. If it helps, just pull up the picture of you and me at tonight's dinner and pretend you are speaking to me," he suggested.

"I might just do that," she admitted exposing her blushing cheeks. "Seeing as I might fly back to New York in a day or two, I might need a reminder of a great friend I just met."

"You're going back to New York already?" Camden asked sounding uneasy.

"Well yes! There would be no need to stay at this point because all of my therapy will be done over the phone. Besides, as much as I pushed my husband Victor away, I really miss him," she admitted out loud for the first time since her departure from him.

"Well I'm sure Victor will be pleased to get his wife back given the great lengths you've taken to keep him away," he added with sarcasm in his voice. "I have to admit though; I will miss you and your company." Sounding genuine with his remarks, Camden knew he needed to switch gears and try to get Mary to stay in town. Even if it was for just a short while longer, he knew he needed a little more time with her. "Come to think of it, you haven't even started your therapy yet so perhaps jetting off back home so quickly might not be in your best interest."

"Not in my best interest? What makes you say that? Mary's curiosity was rather peeked given the statement Camden presented. Secretly, she was hoping to have some kind of reasonable excuse to stay for a little while longer, and Camden might have just offered it to her. As much as she missed her husband, there was something about Camden that she found captivating. His strong presence and authentic personality gave luster to their budding friendship. She could tell he too was wounded which peaked her interest in wanting to find out more about him.

"Oh look, our dinner is here," he softly announced, pulling the attention away from her travel plans back home.

"This looks divine." Her eyes widened as each platter was placed on their table. Mary could feel her stomach grumbling harder and louder with every aroma that passed her place setting. She never realized how famished she had become while waiting for the meal to arrive. The aroma alone sent her saliva glands into overdrive. The timing of the food's arrival couldn't have come at a better time. Mary could feel the effects of the wine already, and the night was still young. "This food looks delectable but Mr. Camden; you never answered my question as to why you think I need to stay in Toronto longer."

After clearing his throat and the much needed food distraction, Camden was able to consider his reasons for blurting out a request for her to stay. "Isn't it obvious?" he asked. "You haven't even had a telephone session yet and you've got yourself booked on the next flight out. What if the doctor decides he does indeed need to see you in his office before continuing with your therapy?"

"Well then I guess I will just have to take the next flight back into Toronto," Mary snidely said. "More importantly, would it be all that bad to see my face again because you know I will be calling you to come for a visit."

"No, not bad at all but I still think you should wait and have at least a few sessions with the doctor first before skipping out. You know, just to make sure you're comfortable with him as well," he added. "And just to be clear, it's never a bad thing for me to see your face," he offered flashing his best flirtatious smile.

"You make some very reasonable points for me to stay but I'm not sure why you're so passionate about it," she replied.

"If all goes to plan tonight, I will get to show you how passionate I really am," he blurted out regretting his words the very moment they left his lips.

"Excuse me?" Mary asked sounding confused. Her natural instincts told her to immediately put up an invisible wall so she could shield herself emotionally from this almost stranger she chose to dine with. Another part of her enjoyed the lavish attention and deep seeded fervour he seemed to transmit toward her. Mary couldn't put her finger on it but something in her wanted to figure him out. There was so much more about him she wanted to learn. He seemed to be missing something. There was more to his story and Mary could tell something wasn't jiving with Camden. This unknown element gave her an uneasy feeling about him but yet she trusted him enough to override her own anxiety. As if to test the waters, Mary played along hoping her sudden uncomfortable feelings was just the wine going to her head.

"I'm just joking around," Camden offered as an excuse for his misjudged words.

"Oh, well that's too bad. I'm looking forward to witnessing more of this passion you have to show me," she revealed with a slight slur. Mary was just finishing her third glass of Prosecco when she realized the alcohol was starting to hit her harder than expected. On a normal evening out, three glasses of wine would have her feeling slightly tipsy but Mary felt different this time. Her body tingled and with every breath she could feel her light headiness amplify. Mary excused herself to the ladies room to allow herself to freshen up. Like a true gentleman, Camden rose to her side to assist with her chair. He watched as she staggered away from the table. He could tell that she was concentrating on every step she took trying not to twist her ankle in the very high heels she chose to wear. Once out of his sight, Camden pulled his cell phone out only to be greeted by a waiting text message from Victor. It was no surprise to Camden that Victor was anxious for an update on what was happening with his wife. Keeping his fears and anxiety to a minimum, Camden replied back to Victor ensuring that Mary was safe. Camden even revealed that her therapy appointment was booked with Doctor Copeland for the morning and that Victor shouldn't worry because her appointment was with one of the best doctor in Ontario. He was careful to only give Victor just enough information to keep him satisfied. Victor had no idea Camden changed his last name years ago. An attempt to leave his bitter past behind and start a new life. Camden also omitted the fact that Mary's therapy would be over the telephone; an important piece of information he methodically kept out. Camden didn't want Victor pushing for her to get back home. He repeated that there was nothing Victor should be worried about and that he would send another text later that evening to recap. Pleased with himself, Camden put his cellular phone away and ordered dessert and a nightcap for when Mary arrived back to the table.

~23~

He had been waiting by his phone with great concern for what seemed to be hours on end. Finally when the long anticipated incoming message alert rang out, Victor felt a slight relief from his growing worry. Not knowing where Mary was or how she was doing would sure to be the death of him. Of course he was eager to hear from Camden about Mary's plans and recent interactions but to his surprise, he learned that Mary did indeed make an appointment for treatment. Victor let out the largest sigh of his life. He could almost feel the physical worry vibrate past his lips as the hot air dissipated directly in front of his face. A long overdue grin grew upon his recent pale and unshaven face for the first time in over a week. He sat back on his overstuffed couch and sank into the comforting leather allowing his cell phone to slip from his hand and drop adjacent to him. The relief he felt was long overdue. His built up worry and stress proved to have some effects on him. Victor's anxiety attacks and his lack of sleep aged his physical appearance more in one week than his entire over demanding and high stress career had ever done. Feeling less panicked about Mary, Victor knew that he needed his mind and body to rest so he would be rejuvenated for when Mary returned home. He allowed his thoughts and anxiety to settle with each deep breath he took. Taking in the relaxed atmosphere and allowing his body the much needed rest it ached for was his only means of quieting his constant thoughts. Without delay he closed his eyes dipping deep into the complete darkness of his eye lids. The quiet space quickly transformed him into inner peace. He systematically monitored his breathing patterns careful to take deep breaths in through his nose, slowly and steadily exhaling through his mouth. He felt his heart beat calming in his chest with every breath he took. His relaxed state felt so good to him. His tense muscles twitched every so often as they too needed to relax from their constant stiff state. Euphoria quickly engulfed Victor's body as he continued to let his stress melt away. His exhilarated state came to a jolting end as soon as his cell phone rang. Victor jumped up frantically searching for his phone that he allowed to escape from his tight grip. His head felt dizzy as he tried to focus on the caller id. Despite the caller's name glowing through the blue hue on his cell phone face, Victor couldn't get his eyes to focus properly. He wasn't sure how long he rested but by the looks of the evening sky, he was sure at least an hour or so already slipped by. He felt instantly paralyzed when he read the caller was his wife Mary. His heart began to pound rapidly against his chest as he fumbled to press the answer button.

"Hello? Mary?" he said trying to sound calm.

The silence on the other end of the call deafened his ear drums. All he could hear was a slight muffle and the sound of his own heart beat. Unsure as to why she was calling sent Victor into a full blown panic attack.

"Hello? Hello! Hello Mary, are you there?" Victor repetitive said hoping for an answer. Desperate for a response, he found himself pacing the apartment while constantly looking at his cell phone to make sure the call didn't disconnect. He could feel the tiny beads of sweat rippling down his face onto his neck.

"Victor, can you hear me?" Mary repeated.

"I can hear you, I can hear you," he said with a whisper of relief in his voice. "Are you okay?"

"I think so," she admitted. "I feel a little tipsy from the wine I've had tonight but other than that I'm doing great," she confessed.

"Wine, okay so that explains why you're slurring slightly," he said out loud to himself.

Trying to analyse the situation, Victor found his mind thinking of a million things all at once. The lack of concentration left him unable to think straight. The fact that Mary made it entirely clear that she didn't want nor need Victor's help confused his thought process but he welcomed her surprise call. He slapped his cheek a few times to make sure he was not in a dream like state.

"I just wanted to let you know that I've missed you terribly and that I will be coming home in a few days," Mary explained trying hard not to slur.

"That's great news Mary," Victor said with some hesitation. "Are you finished with your therapy?"

Victor knew all too well that her therapy would not be completed in the short duration that she had been away for. In fact, he played down the entire thing knowing he was not supposed to have any information on her what so ever. Mary would lose all trust in him if she found out Victor paid someone to follow her. Victor figured an open statement could lead Mary into a more in depth conversation with him. He wanted to keep her on the phone, long enough to savour the sound of her voice. A long overdue conversation he was hoping would happen sooner rather than later.

"No, my therapy is not finished yet," Mary responded skipping over the fact that it really hadn't even started. "I have the green light to continue therapy over the phone so that leaves me the flexibility to come home."

"That is the best news I have heard all day," he told her. Victor's grin couldn't have been bigger if he tried. He could almost feel his love for her grow deeper within his heart. All he had ever wanted for her was inner peace from her past tortures. Her love, kindness, generosity and vulnerability were all traits he fell deeply in love with but only now something seemed different. Mary's ability to tackle her inner monsters without the assistance of anyone showed Victor how strong she really was. He beamed with joy and one day soon he would be able to tell her how incredibly happy he was for her. For now, Victor had to settle on having to bottle up his excitement and allow Mary to continue on her self help journey alone. Little did Victor know, Mary's only concentration was being able to stand in the bathroom without the assistance of the sink. Her tight grip was the only thing that kept her from falling over. Not wanting to alert Victor, Mary thought it was best to end their conversation before her lack of poor choices on drinking too much was revealed.

"I will need to wrap a few things up before making my way home, but please don't worry about me. I have everything under control," she stated just before she hung up.

Victor could not help but feel completely and utterly exhausted. The fact that Mary was on some sort of road to recovery made her absence all worth it. Knowing that she would be coming home soon put Victor at ease. So much so, he immediately fired off an e-mail to his assistant informing her that he would be returning to work the next day. Work was Victor's life outside of Mary. He felt secure and right at home anytime he stepped foot into his office. He had complete control over every aspect in his office life and that was exactly how he liked to live. Victor was sure that was why he went through so much anxiety while Mary was away. He lost control of her. There was no connection, no input, no direction and no helping with her situation. He had no control over anything she did or decided upon. He immediately felt his heart racing again. The thought of her navigating through any personal problems on her own sent his blood pressure skyrocketing upwards and rapidly. Mary was the only woman who had this affect on him and he knew it from the moment he met her all those years ago.

The morning sun was trying its best to escape the cloud covered sky when the harsh gusts of wind smashed into Victor's bedroom windows startling him from a deep sleep. It had been the first restful night he had since Mary left for her trip back to Toronto. He reached over into the empty side of his king size bed hoping to feel the warmth of Mary's body next to him. As he lay on his side thinking of her; his eyes well adjusted to the start of his work day, he could almost hear her soft breathing. A sound Victor had listened to over and over again for almost ten years. It was the sound that kept him grounded in life. The purpose for his drive and the reason for his deep seeded passion for life. Without her, he would surely be half the man he was today.

~24~

The winds were fierce and unforgiving as daylight entered Mary's hotel suite. The pressure and constant pounding in her head gave life to last night's memories. Mary smiled to herself as she recollected the fun evening of food and drinks. It seemed like forever and a day since she truly let go of all her emotional luggage and just had fun. There was not a worry to be had from her that evening including the dreaded hangover she was now living. Mary couldn't remember much of what happened after her telephone call to Victor but she was not concerned in the least. She was back in her suite, safe and sound. She did however feel slightly off. The nausea she was experiencing was not typical of a night out full of drinking. Mary felt lightheaded and queasy. When she stood up she felt a rush of blood drain from her upper extremities straight down to her feet. After drinking some water, Mary opened her bathroom drawer and removed the pregnancy test she had brought with her from New York. She thought maybe the stress and anxiety from reliving her

Richard nightmare had been the culprit of her queasiness but to be on the safe side, she purchased a pregnancy test. Her plan was to take the pregnancy test while staying in Toronto. She didn't want to give false hope to Victor knowing how much he had dreamt about having a child. When she first arrived in Toronto, Mary wanted to get settled in first before jumping right into a pregnancy test. She was almost certain her upset stomach was caused by her anxiety and nerves. There had been a few days she felt great, mostly when she had been preoccupied by Camden. It seemed like everything was right in her world when Camden was around. So much so, it worried her that her feelings for him might have grown more than what was acceptable and appropriate for a married woman. She found herself smiling and feeling like a giddy school girl whenever she was around him. Last night was no exception. They shared an intimate dinner together full of great conversation and memorable moments of laughter. At one point during their evening together, Mary fantasized what it would be like to kiss him. He was so charming and giving of himself. There were no invisible walls hiding their true identities. She could be herself, her strong independent self around him. Camden was never trying to rescue her from anyone let alone herself. He always allowed her to have her own voice, her own thoughts and make her own decisions. That seemed to be the big difference between him and Victor. She loved Victor whole heartedly but there was this undeniable attraction to Camden she just couldn't put her finger on. The obvious fact that he was good looking came secondary to his persona.

Mary caught a glimpse of herself in the bathroom mirror. Even through last night's makeup, she was glowing. This was the first time in Mary's life she has felt so grounded and put together yet everything in her life was everything but put together. Mary was away from her husband and the home they spent over 9 years building together. She put her career on hold; a career she spent countless hours, days and years growing. She felt like she was falling in love with someone she just met and now there was a possibility that she could be pregnant. There was nothing secure or grounded in her life at the moment, yet she was the happiest she had ever been.

"This is going to be some therapy session today," she muttered to herself.

The adrenalin rush of taking the pregnancy test had her pacing her suite back and forth. Mary was feeling nervous for her first telephone therapy session which exasperated her tense state even more. She tried to pre-script her initial conversation before placing the call to her therapist, but every time she thought she knew what she would say, her thoughts tapered off to the pregnancy test sitting in the bathroom waiting to be read.

"I can't think of that right now," again muttering out loud. "No distraction right now!"

Mary found a comfortable spot on the couch where she envisioned her therapy call to take place. She had already wrapped herself up into a nice warm bathrobe and placed a fresh brewed Camomile Tea on the side table that awaited her attention. All the comfort tools she needed were there at her reach. As she picked up the phone to place the long overdue call, she remembered the picture of her and Camden taken at dinner the night before. She opened the image and stared at it for a moment. She could almost hear his encouraging voice telling her to make the call. As she dialed the Doctor's number, she took in a deep breath and waited. To her surprise, a recording came on explaining the pilot program of telephone therapy. She could only imagine that the recording was protocol and probably had to be done for legality reasons. The recorded voice was that of a female who spoke firm with a steady tone. The professional voice explained the telephone therapy session starting with the session being recorded and that any and all information shared through the untraditional pilot method was the sole property of Doctor Copeland. None of the information would be shared with third parties or sold to agencies. A bunch more legal jargon was spewed to what seemed to be an eternity. Mary quickly lost interest in the recording and was about to hang up when she heard the recording indicating it was redirecting her call to Doctor Copeland. Feeling a little unsettled and still nauseous, Mary straightened up her pose on the couch as if sitting upright would help her sound more professional.

"This is Doctor Copeland, our session is now active. Please indicate your name for recording purposes and we will commence immediately," the doctor instructed.

After clearing her throat, Mary sat back remembering that no one could see her. She placed her cell phone on the speaker mode and retrieved the picture of her and Camden. Looking directly into Camden's eyes that peered back at her through the picture, she found the strength to start her therapy session.

"Um, hello my name is Mary. I live in New York but I'm staying in Toronto right now. I needed some time to clear my head so I came here to my native city where I feel safe and grounded. There has been so much going on that I needed..." Mary continued to ramble.

"Hello Mary," the Doctor interrupted. "Before we get started, I just wanted to acknowledge your strength for seeking therapy. You are in complete control of the dialogue. In fact, you won't be hearing much from me today as I am here to listen. If you ask me a question, I will answer but please know I am not here to judge you. I am here solely to listen and offer unbiased direction in order for you to conquer your troubles. At anytime, should you wish to end the conversation, you can just hang up. I will not call back nor will I place any alerts on your profile. Your confidentiality is safe with this telephone therapy so please feel free to express yourself without concern or duress. This session is 45 minutes long. You will hear a warning sound when there is 5 minutes remaining. At that time, you should attempt to wrap up your thoughts so you can continue for the next session period. Once the session concludes, the call will automatically disconnect regardless of where you are in your sentence. Do you understand these instructions?"

"Yes," she responded trying to retain all the information at once.

"Good! You may proceed when you are ready," he instructed.

"Yes, okay then. Do I start all over again?" she asked unsure of how therapy worked in an office let alone over the phone.

"It's not necessary to start over. Whatever means or direction that helps you feel comfortable talking about what is troubling you will be fine," the doctor said trying to guide her into conversation. "You already mentioned you are from New York but you are staying in Toronto. Are you running away from something?"

"That's a great question Doctor. In fact, I guess I could answer that question with a yes. Only I'm not really running away from one single thing but rather multiple things. When I really think about it, I'm running from my past, my present and possibly my future. You see in my past I was in an abusive relationship only I didn't really know it at the time. He was my first intimate relationship so I didn't know what normal was supposed to be. He tormented me! He was physically abusive. He was mentally abusive and he was verbally abusive. I stayed with him longer than I really should have because I didn't know any better. I was young and naive. He was smart and so charming. He was rich and took care of me while I concentrated on building my career. I relocated my entire life and moved to a different city to be with him. I was alone, scared and inexperienced. I guess I really needed him until my career was strong enough to leave him. I guess that makes me a user to him too. I'm so ashamed of my actions and my choices. I really loved him too which makes it even more difficult to try and wrap my head around it all," Mary spouted before falling silent.

The doctor could hear Mary weep but resisted the urge to ask for more details. With the scattered information she already shared, he sensed there was so much more to her story. He remained silent even though her quiet weeping turned to an unmistakable cry. He could tell she was trying hard to hold back; like most patients, they often felt embarrassed when they exhibited raw emotion. Knowing that Mary was clamming up, the Doctor asked an open ended question to keep the communications flowing.

"You mentioned running away from multiple things and you've touched upon the abuse you've endured. Let's talk about the other things you have been running from as well." The Doctor's tone was so soft and welcoming.

"In a way, I feel like I'm running away from my husband. You see, I purposefully pushed him away and denied his help. All these years together and I've never wanted to talk to him about my troubles. He's always saved me from everything. He was the one who rescued me from the big bad Richard. Listen to me addressing my husband as *he*. As if Victor doesn't deserve the notable recognition for turning my life around. I'm so selfish! I'm so broken! I'm so torn up about so many things. I feel like I'm talking in circles and I'm all over the place. I'm so scrambled," Mary admitted to the doctor and to herself.

"It's okay Mary. You are entitled to be feeling this way. You are not the one at fault. You're doing great, please continue," he coached with his endearing trance like voice.

"I came to Toronto to try and get away from my troubles, instead I feel like I have more troubles now than I started with," she admitted.

"That's a bold statement. What is making you feel that way?" he probed.

Mary took a deep breath in and gave herself time to think carefully about her answer.

"This session is confidential right?" she asked confirming what she already knew.

"Yes. Everything you say will remain confidential. I am held liable by doctor and patient privilege. Please do not place any concern or worry on that matter from here on out. Your spoken words are safe with me. So what are these additional problems you speak of?" he asked trying hard not to sound too pushy.

"Oh my God, where do I even start?" The first thing shouldn't be a problem. It should be a joy but I feel like it complicates everything and I even feel guilty just saying that," Mary continued to ramble.

"Okay, I don't usually interrupt but Mary, you need to slow down and try to regroup your thoughts. Please try to describe what is actually causing you all this stress," the Doctor guided.

"Right! You're right," Mary agreed. "For the past month, I haven't been feeling so great. I mean not just emotionally but physically too. At first I thought maybe I was putting too many hours in at work so I slowed my schedule down. I still felt uneasy and weak. Once I confronted my husband Victor about seeking therapy I thought I would start feeling better. You know the anxiety of leaving your husband and your home can play havoc in your head but there was no relief like I expected there to be. Once I arrived in Toronto I felt slightly better but I have to admit, I was still very tired. I chalked that up to travel. The next day, I planned for some shopping and me time which I admit did make me feel better. I'm pretty sure my company had something to do with me feeling good," Mary instantly smiled.

"Company? The doctor instantaneously sounded intrigued. "Who is this company you speak of?"

"I became friends with my taxi driver. His name is Camden and he's really nice, Mary proudly announced.

"Go on," the doctor said clearly showing interest.

"He's really been there for me. We've practically spent every day together since I arrived in Toronto. He's charming you know? It's like he really gets me. My husband gets me too but Camden doesn't smother me, or at least I don't feel like he does. There's no expectations or ties to one another, just genuine friendship.

"Do you feel like your husband smothers you?" the doctor digs for more information.

"No! Well kind of…yes. You see, Victor inadvertently treats me like a small helpless child. He's always so worried about my emotional state; he doesn't realize when he acts like that he pushes me further away from him. I feel like there is no room to breathe, to grow and to understand why I can't seem to let go of some of my past events. He always tries to get me to talk about what's bothering me," she admitted trying to dig deeper into her true feelings.

"Do you not feel comfortable speaking to him about your life events?" Doctor Copeland asked.

"My life events," Mary said with laughter. "That's a great positive way to position it. I have spoken to him about them, a few years ago. I really opened up about some of the terrible things that happened to me. I let myself be vulnerable and in turn, Victor became more protective of me," Mary explained.

"You speak as if you find Victor's attempts to offer you safety and security to be a negative quality. Do you feel that someone offering you protection prohibits you in being a successful person?" the doctor asked bluntly. "Or are you more concerned about allowing your vulnerability to show leading to more emotional enclosure?

"No, that's not what I'm trying to say at all," Mary verbalized with a ting of frustration emanating through. "What I'm trying to say without sounding like a feminist is that I don't need any man protecting me from my own thoughts or the big bad world we live in."

The five minute warning sound could clearly be heard from both parties in conversation. Deep into thought and nowhere near finished with spilling her frustration in order to clear her head space, Mary chose to ignore the warning beep.

"I'm so messed up right now, I can't even think straight and now I feel so rushed with this session. Who invented this warning beep anyway?" she asks clearly unable to ignore its meaning and growing more flustered by the rushed moments.

"It's very unconventional of me to allow a session to supersede its allotted time but in this very rare incidence I will allow it and only because I don't feel comfortable wrapping up this session when you feel so dishevelled," the doctor explained.

"I do appreciate your kindness Doctor Copeland and I assure you that I can handle my distractions but with that being said, I am thankful because I have a few more concerns that I just want to get off my chest today," she continued.

Doctor Copeland leaned back into his seat feeling quite pleased with himself. Although extending a therapy session was not unheard of, most doctors didn't allow for that extra time in their schedules. Part of being a good therapist was being able to accommodate a client for their session especially when it was a new client. Doctor Copeland's practice always strived on treating patients with the utmost confidentiality and practicality. Some of his long time patients took advantage but most were just grateful for his understanding of their needs. Doctor Copeland's character proved to be indomitable enough to keep his practice running smoothly while allowing his patients to feel in control of their own therapy needs. That's how he conducted all his therapy sessions, up until a few years ago. Allowing Mary extra time in her session gave the doctor more information than even he expected to hear.

"I told my husband that I was coming home but now I'm not so sure I want to do that or even if it's the right thing to do right now," she admitted.

"Why do you feel that it may not be the right thing to do?" Doctor Copeland asked.

"It's so complicated. Victor's has always been my safety net but I feel ridiculed in a way because of that. He's so rich and powerful and can take care of anything, including his broken wife. I don't want to be looked after anymore like a kept woman. I want to be free and untroubled, just like Camden makes me feel," she said.

As the bold confession slipped from her mouth, she could feel the crushing anxiety of her internalized feelings ooze out from deep inside. After ten years of internalizing her emotions and what she felt was the ultimate and perfect marriage at the time, Mary allowed the growth to her analytical thoughts that had been surfacing for some time to finally escape. Her unexplained child like behaviour appeared to have surfaced as a way to push back from the only man in her life that protected her. Her sense of entrapment and feelings of suffocation was the result of Victor's overprotective goodwill. It was her only reasonable explanation for why she was developing feelings for another man. A man she hardly knew but desperately felt she needed and wanted to know better.

The relief of those drowning thoughts gave new life to her next inhaled breath. Without skipping a beat more truth flooded the doctor's ear.

"I think I have fallen in love with this guy Camden I just met," Mary confided. Mary tensed up almost holding her breath unsure of what the doctor would say.

"Please go on and take your time. There is no need to rush. I can understand your confusion. Has this Camden fella reciprocated on your feelings?" the doctor guided in a comforting tone.

"He's very kind and understanding with me. I'm still getting to know him but I can feel the connection between us. It's like he doesn't want to overstep the boundary because he knows I'm married which I respect but it only makes me want to pursue him more. Like the cat and mouse game you know? Only he's the mouse and I'm the cat chasing him. I know it's wrong.

It's wrong for me to have these feeling but I have them and it's tearing me up. To make matters worse, I think I'm pregnant," she revealed to the doctor; unconscious of the fact that he was the first person she told. "I just took a home pregnancy test before I called you."

Remembering that the pregnancy test was still sitting on the washroom counter waiting for the results to be read, she rushed into the bathroom with her cell phone in hand.

"Let me change my statement from *might be* pregnant to the test is positive," she announced.

"Pregnant! Yes, I understand why this would cause some confusion in your life," he articulated trying to remain as professional as he could.

"Some confusion is a big understatement. Now I'm more confused than ever," she admitted.

"Okay listen Mary, I know this is not the best time for us to end this therapy session but I assure you that you can call me anytime today should you feel the need to talk more about this. I think it would serve you well to do some silent thinking and perhaps you will be able to find answers to some of your confusion. Some of the best solutions come to those who meditate without distraction. I want you to go and meditate quietly by yourself, preferably in a nearby park and let nature sooth your thoughts.

Remember to take deep breaths in and slowly exhale to release all your confusion. Let's pick this up again tomorrow when your thoughts have had time to filter through their confused state," Doctor Copeland concluded.

Without waiting for Mary's response, he ended the session call.

~25~

Feeling like a fresh new man, Victor woke up to the most amazing idea and he just couldn't hold his excitement together any longer. Arranging for a private helicopter to pick Mary up from Toronto was only the first of his many surprises he had planned for her. Not only was he excited to be getting his wife back home, but having her home in time to celebrate Halloween together was the icing on the cake. Remembering their Bonnie and Clyde costumes, Victor thought it would be humorous to pick her up in full costume. Halloween was Victor's favourite time of year. He never missed an opportunity to celebrate the cherished children's holiday and found the concept of dressing up only to act in incognito for the night to be riveting. Mary was sure to be surprised, not only by his arrival but also by his decadent choice of attire. She never fully invested herself into the holiday but went along with Victor's love for the character indulgence. After all, their costumes were always a coupled theme and Victor took care of the details. There was nothing for Mary to do other than have fun at the party.

Victor arranged for the private helicopter to be on standby for whenever he needed it. There wasn't much more he needed to attend to in order for that part to run smoothly. A quick phone call to set a departure time was the last thing he needed to take care of. The only obstacle that could put his plan in jeopardy was the timing of his arrival to pick Mary up. He knew he had to have a solid plan. Getting Camden in on the plan was the only way to ensure everything could run smoothly. Camden's been the one constant person allowing Victor to remain somewhat in charge. After sending a text to Camden instructing him to call immediately, Victor waited patiently to complete the last few details of his plan. Picking Mary up by four o'clock that afternoon would leave them enough time to fly back to New York and attend the Halloween Gala for the Homeless and Hungry. Giving back to their city was a top priority in Victor and Mary's lives. Victor was known for being a dispassionate attorney, but his more humane side allowed him to dedicate his knowledge and money to more practical and worthy causes. Victor was the perfect blend of professional mannerism with a hint of being self focused. His desire to help others often ruled his better judgement and that was exactly how he landed a seat on the Gala's board of directors. With his passion for people and his love of Halloween, the Halloween Gala for the Homeless and Hungry was born. This year's second annual Gala and the return of Mary couldn't have been timed any better. Ironically Bonnie and Clyde would be giving back to their community instead of taking as the classic tale was once told.

Victor fumbled to answer his cell phone as he clumsily dropped his costume hat. Still reminiscing about his Gala he answered the call still in character. "Least I ain't a liar," he said in his best Clyde impersonating twang voice.

"A Liar?" Camden started.

"Hey, sorry man I was just rehearsing some of my lines for tonight's Gala event..." Victor tried to explain.

"Okay, whatever. Listen, I'm in a little bit of a hurry, I'm returning your call so can you make this quick?" Camden shoots.

"Quick! Yes, me too funny enough. I need Mary's hotel information. I've got the best surprise for her," Victor announced with excitement.

"She's still at the Four Seasons Hotel in Yorkville," he blurted out clearly distracted by something other than the phone call.

"That's great," Victor replied sounding both amused and enlightened to finally confirm her whereabouts. "Make sure she's there at four o'clock today to receive her surprise," Victor ordered and ended his call.

"Four o'clock, yes of course," Camden replied to the dial tone still distracted by his own thoughts.

Victor arranged a black car service for his arrival at Million Air municipal airport. The small Toronto Airport facility allowed private jets and helicopters from around the world to utilize their fixed base operation. It was exactly what Victor needed. Besides the fact that most people did not travel in costume, Victor and his Clyde costume was sure to get some unwelcoming looks from other travelers at the large international airport. He also didn't want any hardship from customs with his toy gun that was clearly visible and tucked into his pants. Victor just wanted to wrangle up his Bonnie and bring her home in time for the Gala.

Victor paced his apartment walking from room to room rendering his thoughts of how he was going to approach Mary for the first time in three weeks. Would she think he had completely lost his mind showing up at her suite in a Clyde costume? Clearly she would remember that it was Halloween. It was one of the best days of the year in Victor's opinion. The only day of the year where civilized people got to dress up in personified characters and everyone was okay with it. Mary would be okay with it too. Victor was certain that when she saw him in his costume, she would want to put on her Bonnie costume and support the worthy cause alongside him.

With little time to waste, Victor connected his cell phone up to his laptop so he could run a backup as well as dump all of the phone's content. The evening's Gala was scheduled to have almost twice the amount of attendees than last year and Victor wanted to ensure he had more than enough memory on his cell to capture all the great memories. He also hoped in doing a backup on his phone, it would stop glitching. Over the past week Victor noticed his phone lagging as well as dropping calls. The IT specialist at his office recommended a backup and re-boot of his device. Victor wanted to make certain that nothing interrupted or ruined his evening especially since it would be the first evening he got to spend with his wife in over three weeks. Following the on screen instructions, Victor waited patiently for his thousands of pictures and videos to upload into his computer backup drive. Smiling and adoring at every picture that flashed on his screen, Victor watched as the memories trickled into the backup file. It helped make the time pass quicker. There were so many pictures, so many good times. The picture flashbacks enhanced his deep desire to want to hold Mary in his arms once again. Victor had always found it so easy to love her. Mary's gallant façade is what attracted others to her but Victor knew her like no other man ever could. He witnessed her insecurities and cradled her deepest fear; protecting her from the cruel realities of the unsympathetic world they lived in. Victor's benevolent character was the perfect match to her scarred soul. Nearly ten years ago when they united, Victor and Mary both vowed nothing and no one would crumble their unity. They promised each other a life filled with trust, honesty, devotion and unfiltered affection.

Snapping back to the present moment, Victor's device alerted him that his upload was complete. He immediately rebooted his phone to complete the process in anticipation of leaving for the airport to pick up his love. The minutes felt like hours, dragging on like a poorly written opera. Victor poured himself a small shot of brandy as he eagerly waited for the final reboot moments. To his great excitement, his cell phone sounded with an e-mail alert followed by a text message. As Victor fervently retrieved his phone from the desktop, another text alert sounded. Curious as to who was texting, he ignored the e-mail and went straight to reading his text. Victor's face turned a slight hue of red followed by a pale white. Slumping into his desk chair, he could not believe what he was seeing. The smug look on Camden's face told an entire story of its own. Picture after picture exposed an even riskier and scantily clad pose of the man Victor once knew as a good friend. The last picture was the one that felt like a knife stuck through him. The look on his wife's face was supremely innocent as she lay in her hotel bed, eyes closed in the arms of another man. Not just any man though. The one man Victor entrusted with his most precious gift was the same man clutching onto his wife. Not only was Camden an old school friend who Victor thought he could trust they were also long time friends. They were going to become the best lawyers New York had ever seen. Camden wasn't just any friend; he was a close friend of Victor's who journeyed through an educational dream of becoming a lawyer. There were even talks and aspirations of starting their own practice together. Sure they lost track of each other for a number of years when Camden decided to pursue another career avenue but that didn't mean Victor forgot about their friendship and the strong bond they built. He was the same friend who had no problem accepting a paying position to keep a woman safe and out of harm's way. Not just a random woman but Victor's wife.

Victor stared at the pictures unsure of how to control his mixed emotions. He wanted nothing more than to smack that smug smirk off Camden's face. The way he was staring back in the picture was almost staged and deliberate. Was this the victory picture he finally got the guts to send? Why did Mary have her eyes closed? Was she blinking at that very moment or had she fallen asleep? Did she even know he took this picture? Was this new relationship the reason why Mary decided to come home earlier than originally planned? Was Mary going to leave him for this chump of a so called friend? Victor couldn't help but question every last detail of the pictures. He started to think that maybe he deserved what he has getting, seeing as he went behind Mary's back and hired Camden to spy on her. Victor never meant to be sneaky or snide; he just tried to build a platform of protection for her. A safeguard by proxy to ensure Mary's protection was all Camden was supposed to be. Victor found it difficult to keep his emotions in check while trying to think rationally about the whole situation. It didn't make sense that Camden would randomly send pictures to him. Did he send them by mistake? Victor's worst fears were coming to life. The next text message from Camden was the worst one yet.

"I hope you enjoyed the pictures I sent earlier. As promised, I've kept your wife safe and very, very happy. Soon enough she will be mine…your good friend, Camden."

Victor could almost hear Camden's words vibrating off of his lips, emitting an undertone of evil bait. The dark tone of his text gave Victor all the evidence he needed to get on that private helicopter and rescue his wife from the clasp of Camden's malevolence. Any doubts Victor may have had about his travels to Toronto were quickly abolished the second he received the malice texts from Camden. The pictures and taunting words solidified his uneasy feelings about Mary's trip. Victor's harsh anxiety spells and the ongoing gut wrenching uneasy feelings were the universe sending out subliminal rescue messages, and now it all made sense to him. He always listened to his instincts, both in the courtroom and in his personal life. Why he didn't act on them sooner was something Victor would need to answer to at a later date. His first priority was to board the private helicopter and rescue the love of his life.

~26~

Mary stared at the pregnancy test for what seemed to be an eternity. Trying hard to clear her mind of all thoughts, Mary shoved the pregnancy test in her purse and grabbed a small blanket out of the hall closet. She needed to get to the park and meditate, just like the doctor suggested. She couldn't think of a better option to help clear head. As she walked along the bustling sidewalk, Mary couldn't help but allow her thoughts to penetrate through the news of her pregnancy. She knew how elated Victor would be with the news of having a child. Although she never expressed a yearning to have children herself, Mary was excited at the prospect of becoming a mother. After Victor and Mary wed, they had conversations about enjoying their marriage and careers for a few years before starting a family. With their tenth year anniversary fast approaching, Mary was excited to be celebrating both a decade of marriage and a new child. She envisioned giving a proper pregnancy announcement to all her guests at the anniversary party, allowing her guests to celebrate the joyous occasion together.

It wasn't difficult to find some beautiful green space in the luxurious streetscape of Yorkville. Most streets in that area had picturesque grass space surrounded with office towers, perfect for the working professionals to enjoy some fresh air and outdoor lunching. More often than not, most office personnel in the area would take advantage of the good weather and tuck themselves under an unusually large tree to sneak in some reading time or even partaking in some office e-mail catch up. Anyone walking along the tree lined street could easily witness the beauty of the peaceful atmosphere. A simple escape from a frenzied day was exactly what the space was designed for. After choosing her perfect spot, Mary spread her blanket out onto the grass. She starred up into the beautiful blue sky trying hard to come up with a special way to tell Victor he was going to be a dad. Mary was certain Victor would agree that having children at this stage in their marriage would be indicative to the love they share for each other. Ten years was a good run for a couple to enjoy marriage before adding to their family, considering divorce rates were higher than ever. Mary wasn't sure if she was trying to convince herself of motherhood or if her hormones where already kicking into hypersensitive mode. Whatever the reality of their current feelings on the matter was, the fact still remained the same. Mary was pregnant with Victor's child. Any and all feelings she thought she may have experienced toward Camden had to come to an end. More than ever Mary knew she needed to get back to her home and share the unexpected and great news with her husband. It was time for her to put her big girl pants on and wake up to the reality of her life. Sometimes bad things happen to good people and Mary could clearly see her path into the future now. The clouds and fog that were hovering in her head have all cleared and it was time to put her past into the past and leave it there. Why did it take so long for her to realize that she already had everything that life had to offer? Why did she feel like she was missing a part of herself? Richard may have robbed her of her innocence but he could never take away her willingness to heal and move on from it. Everything seemed crystal clear to Mary now. It was like her life path was illuminated by the news of her pregnancy. Her desire to become a mother was stronger than anything she had ever felt in her life. Maybe the news of her pregnancy was the internal hollowness she couldn't get over and never really knew how to, until now. Could it be that motherhood was the answer to clearing her continuous feelings of sorrow and pulsing heartache that she just couldn't run from anymore?

Mary knew she had to get to her psychologist office right away and fill him in on her new revelation. Getting back home to Victor was the highest of her priorities but first she had to speak to Dr. Copeland and explain the urgency for her immediate departure. Mary remembered Dr. Copeland telling her that she could call anytime if she needed further therapy but this situation was different. She had to go see him in the flesh. Mary knew leaving would require a face to face explanation as to why she felt the urgent need to get back home to Victor. She didn't want to leave without explaining her unequivocal love and bond she shared with her husband. After careful deliberation and sensory evaluation, Mary was certain that her misleading feelings for Camden were purely hormone induced. A particularly important topic she needed to clear up before her departure back home. She thought about the different ways to approach Camden about her falsified feelings toward him but none of the explanations seemed genuine. She figured the proper words would start to flow naturally from her lips the moment she saw him, but first she needed to get to Doctor Copeland's office. A call to Camden would come secondary.

The fall winds were starting to pick up leaving Mary with a frigid chill down her back. The thin cashmere cardigan she picked out earlier didn't seem to keep the cold winds from piercing her skin. Desperate to get out of the cold front that was quickly moving in, Mary hailed a cab at the nearest streetscape. The taxicab driver was soft spoken and questionably young, but she would quickly learn that he'd been driving cab straight out of high school. A questionable career choice for most young enthusiastic men eager to spread their wings in the big world but Steven didn't have much of a choice. He grew up in the city with his parents and younger sister. When his father fell ill and couldn't work anymore, Steven swiftly took the role of income earner and family provider. He never showed any signs of regret or animosity for the role he was forced into; instead he remained grateful for his opportunity at a good wage.

It had started to rain as they approached Doctor Copeland's office building. Mary had never felt so nervous in her life, not even when she left New York on her own to find answers and resolution to her inner turmoil. It was as though she knew this moment in time would be the most important passage of her life. She wasn't sure why, but she knew without a doubt what she was about to do would ultimately change her life forever.

Mary settled the fare with Steven the cab driver and watched him drive off. She stalled for just a little more time to put her thoughts together. Still unsure of how to start the conversation with Doctor Copeland, Mary knew it had to be done regardless of her uncertain approach. As she stepped inside the office tower, she felt an uneasy twinge roll through her center core. She chalked it up to nerves and not knowing what she was going to say to the Doctor upon her unexpected and surprise visit. Mary wasn't even sure he would be there but it was worth her try. As she stood in the lobby of his office building, Mary contemplated on leaving without saying a word but she knew turning back was not an option. The lobby felt hallow and damp, unusual for a professional office building. She proceeded to the large lobby directory that hung adjacent to the concierge desk that no one occupied. Mary paused after reading every section on the board, unable to locate the name of Doctor Copeland. Startled by the nice looking and well dressed men approaching her direction, Mary jumped back to allow them to pass. She could feel her knees tremble as they made their way closer. The men were strong and appeared to be powerful; definitely breathtaking which made Mary blush at the sight of them. She could tell there was a solid camaraderie among them, a feeling she has witnessed with Victor since the inception of their relationship. She observed some of the gentlemen eyeing her but they said nothing, instead they kept their conversation among themselves. She stood watching them quietly, unaccompanied, wondering if they might know who Doctor Copeland was. She found herself mesmerized by one gentleman in particular. He seemed to stand out in the bunch, projecting almost a whole foot taller than the rest; wearing a navy blue Armani suit paired with tan ostrich skinned Prada shoes. The men could pass as a group of lawyers but nowhere on the directory board did it indicate a law office. The information board was littered with doctors varying in different fields and specialties but no lawyers to speak of. The tallest gentleman looked to be of European decent with his thick dark wavy hair and his equally lush facial hair offering an ideal midnight shadow to accompany his professional look. Mary couldn't stop staring at him. His model like physique gave him a dignified presence much like the men he stood with only it was obvious the others respected his opinion and guidance. The men encircled his every move and offered praise and laughter with every sentence that left his mouth. Although

Mary could not hear what they were saying, she knew their discourse was serious. Startled by the concierge attendant shuffling paperwork from behind the tall desk, Mary inquired about which office space Doctor Copeland occupied. She cleared her throat and tried hard to keep her irresolute voice from cracking.

"Can I help you?" the gentleman behind the concierge desk asked softly. His seemingly gentle tone offered an invitation to speak without hesitation. Mary felt comfortable immediately after hearing his whispering voice allowing all her built up fear to diminish.

"Yes you can," she said without pause. "Please direct me to the office of Doctor Copeland; he is expecting me."

"Doctor Copeland," he repeated. First to make sure he had heard the name correctly, secondly to keep the name fresh in his mind while he searched the computer for the name.

"I'm terribly sorry for interrupting you but I didn't notice his name on the directory board," Mary explained hoping she wasn't at the wrong office building.

"No trouble at all," he assured. "I'm not showing a current listing for a Doctor Copeland, but let me just check something else out first."

"Is there something wrong?" she inquired feeling slightly uneasy about meeting with Doctor Copeland without a formal appointment. Mary was certain she had the proper address but the constant clacking on the computer keyboard told her another story. The concierge was clearly having difficulty finding the doctor's name on the office registry list which only added to Mary's uneasy feeling about the whole thing.

"You did say Doctor Copeland correct?" he inquired just to be sure.

"Yes that's right. He is a psychologist if that helps in any way," she adds.

"No, well yes it clarifies that I have the right doctor but I'm sorry to inform you that the doctor is no longer occupying his office space here anymore. Our records indicate that he was occupying office 704 but there is no clear date of release from the occupant." The young man read out loud sounding confused from the information he was reading directly from his own computer screen.

"So Doctor Copeland no longer has office space here? Is that what you're telling me?" Mary clarified trying to make sense of what she was hearing.

"Technically the doctor's office space has been discharged from our directory but as far as I can tell, Doctor Copeland still remains the occupant of the space," the concierge explained hoping it made more sense to Mary than it did to him.

He continued to click on the computer keyboard in hopes to finding a better explanation to offer her. The obvious look of confusion on Mary's face made him want to dig deeper into the doctor's file to help clarify the reason for his office directory disappearance.

There was a long moment of silence when neither one of them spoke a word. Mary considered running to the stairwell as fast as she could but she knew that her shoe choice for the day wouldn't allow for such a sprint. Besides, Mary was sure the concierge would understand if she wanted to go up to the office space to check it out. Maybe she could even concoct a quick witted story about Doctor Copeland subleasing the space to her and wanting to just take a peek at the square footage.

"Doctor Copeland does indeed have space here. The Doctor continues to pay for the occupied space but his practice had been removed from the directory board for reasons unknown. This type of thing happens sometimes, and it's usually because of legal issues surrounding the Doctor's practice or because the office has relocated and the unlisted space is being used strictly for record keeping," he tells Mary while still deep into searching information on his computer. "If you don't mind, I'm just going to Google his name to see if anything on the topic comes up for better clarity."

"That's okay, it's really not necessary to search why he's off the directory list. All I know is that I have a quick meeting with him and I'm a little pressed for time. I have a plane to catch back to New York in a few hours and I have to get a few more things done before I leave."

Mary was relieved to discover that his office was indeed still located in the office tower. Why he wasn't on the registry wasn't a concern to her anymore. Her main worry was to set a few things straight in what she let slip in their last conversation as well as to assure the doctor that her choice in going back to New York was in fact the proper thing for her to do. Reuniting with Victor and sharing the news of their baby was all she wanted to concentrate on.

"What's the office number again?" she asked. "I'd like to quickly run up to say my goodbye and then I'll be off."

"My records indicate that he occupied suite 704. Please take the elevator on the far left over there past the group of gentlemen," he responded pointing to his left.

Releasing personal information about an occupant were grounds for immediate dismissal. He wanted nothing more than to get Mary on her way so he wouldn't get caught sharing the personal information. The disapproving glance from the tall business man on the other side of Mary offered a warning that was unmistakably noticeable.

Mary concluded that the group of men congregating in the lobby were most likely shareholders of the building. The undeniably good looking tall one could be the majority shareholder but either way, he did not seem impressed to hear the concierge leak the private occupant information.

"Thank you for your assistance Glen," Mary squinted her eyes over exaggerating the fact that she was reading off his name tag. "Please have yourself a great day."

"Likewise I'm sure," Glen said with an embarrassing squeak that sounded like air slowing seeping out of a balloon. Knowing that he would be receiving a second reprimand in as many months, Glen instantly felt regret for his misdemeanor.

Mary made her way to the elevator on the left just as she was directed by the now nervous concierge. Purposefully allowing her elbow to brush up against the fine looking lad who occupied much of her thoughts for the past twenty minutes, Mary flirtatiously brushed her hair over her left shoulder exposing a glimpse of her cleavage. In a small way, she hoped her innocent act of cleavage distraction would direct the business man's thoughts onto a more interesting topic. Clearly, she understood the business perspective in keeping client information confidential but Glen really didn't release a terrible amount of personal information to her. Mary's frivolous action of flirtation made her feel better about getting the information she needed and hopefully the right amount of distraction to take the heat off of the concierge, even for just a moment.

~27~

His flight left on time and according to plan. Victor sat patiently in his seat awaiting his arrival to Toronto. He envisioned teleportation and only wished it was something that existed in real time. Allowing his brain to concentrate on other topics proved useful in helping pass the time on his short flight. Victor couldn't stand the thought of Camden remotely standing close to Mary after witnessing the disgusting text messages he received earlier. Every time Victor looked at the images on his cell phone, he held back small bursts of bile. The foul aftertaste wasn't punishment enough for allowing Mary into the dangerous hands of Camden. Victor couldn't shake the deep resentment he was experiencing; after all it was he who pushed Mary into the contemptible arms of Camden to begin with. Had he just left matters alone, Mary would not have encountered Camden. Victor wouldn't be losing his wife to an ex friend clearly suffering from some sort of breakdown. Victor's unsuccessful attempts to reach Mary by phone proved useless for she changed her cell number just as she threatened. His attempt to get the new number from Mary's secretary was futile even though Victor explained the emergency situation. His failed attempts at guessing the safe word Mary had previously set up made it nearly impossible to get her new cell number released from her overly responsive secretary. Mary was sure to set up every obstacle possible knowing how ruthless Victor could be when it came to protecting her.

Victor reviewed his past text conversations with Camden hoping to discover an anomaly of any kind but he kept coming up empty handed. Suffering in the hands of the unknown was the most lonesome place to be. Victor began to understand the torment Mary endured for all those years. He understood all the uncertainties of the 'what if's' and 'how come' simulation now affecting his current life. What if he had forbid Mary to go to Toronto and how come she was so adamant on doing this on her own? Was it possible that Camden orchestrated the entire situation from its inception? Would Mary even go along with such an elaborate plan? Was that the reason for not wanting contact while she settled her inner demons so far away from home? Victor closed his eyes, rested his head on the helicopter backrest and took in a deep breath.

The answers to all of his nonsensical questions would be exposed soon and Victor was looking forward to it.

Victor felt the sky's instability, creating jolting turbulence forcing the helicopter to sway. He reminisced about his last flight with Mary only a short while ago. He could almost feel her hand gripping onto his as the aircraft gave way to the sudden and unpredictable air movements. If Mary was with him right now, she would certainly throw up. His own stomach was twisting with every rigid and jolting dip the helicopter took. The revolting feeling could have solely been brought on by his inner guilt of placing Mary into the hands of Camden himself but he was sure the wrestling flight was adding to his nausea.

The turbulent ride reminded him of his past year of unpredictable change. Work pressure compiled with his strong apprehension of Mary traveling alone gave room for another panic attack but somehow Victor managed to keep his anxiety in check. More now than ever, he needed to be able to think with a clear mind, allowing his thoughts to filter through every situation in hopes to being equipped with a proper resolution. His plan to seek out Camden in person would be the most optimal situation. A face to face meeting would allow Victor the opportunity to confront Camden. He hoped that he could keep his emotions internalized but knew the mere sight of Camden could drive him into a frenzied fit. Victor envisioned hitting him square in the nose knocking him down with one punch but not before shaking an explanation out of him first. Who in their right mind sends their supposed friend a text of themselves being intimate with that person's wife? Victor took out his phone and pulled up the picture of Camden and Mary lying in bed together. The image sent Victor's blood pressure up to abnormal levels almost instantly. He couldn't help but analyze the image. Taking in every detail of the picture was hard for him to do but he had to try and make sense of it. As much as Victor's heart was pounding, he couldn't help but notice how relaxed Mary appeared and how tight and clenched Camden seemed. If they were both sleeping soundly then why would Camden wake to take a picture of them both? If they were having a whirlwind romance, wouldn't Mary be awake and smiling in the picture basking in the love bed of happiness together with him? Why did it seem like Camden staged the picture, almost as if he knew he wanted to use the image for a later date? Something just seemed to be off, or maybe Victor was just grasping at straws that just weren't there.

"Excuse me sir, please turn the volume on your headset. We are getting ready to descend," the pilot informed Victor rattling him back to reality.

"Thank you, I will," he politely responded.

The winds had died down leaving no turbulence to be felt. The landing was quick and seemingly smooth. There was no hand clapping upon touching ground as Victor usually experienced on commercial flights. He looked around the craft and quickly remembered he was on a chartered helicopter. Everything about his day so far was uncharacteristic of his everyday life. He thought at some point in his day he would experience a crowd jump out directly in front of him to announce he'd been punked but so far nothing of the sort had happened.

He was still thinking about Mary when he got into the waiting black car prearranged for his arrival. The comfort of the leather seats hugged and cradled his cold body. The warmth of the heated seats offered ease to his aching back, and he sank into the seat hoping the comfort would also ease his worried mind. Victor questioned if the woman he fell in love over a decade ago would be relieved to see him or would he be walking into heartache far worse than he was willing to accept. He needed her far more than she needed him only Victor never let that fact be known. He never wanted to sound desperate. Victor hated the thought of ever losing Mary let alone to another man, but the reality might be more real than he was willing to face. Victor pictured Mary telling him that she wanted a life of her own, and with Camden. Victor rolled the words around in his head several times but each time he repeated them to himself they sounded more and more peculiar. He wanted to mentally prepare himself for whatever Mary and Camden threw at him, including telling him his marriage was over. He didn't want to believe it, and he was optimistic about having a positive outcome. After all, he hadn't even heard from Mary yet. The last time they spoke she confessed that she missed him and that she was coming home. So why now did Camden send those cruel and disturbing texts? Things were not adding up and Victor couldn't make sense of any of it. The only thing Victor could rely on at the moment was that no matter what he did from here on out, things were going to happen as they should. Although he didn't understand what was happening, he just knew that things would work out the way they were meant to. Just like death. The outcome of death could never be changed. Death was final and there was no coming back from it. Victor would have to treat his marriage to Mary as a death in order to survive divorce. If she tells him that she wants to start a life with Camden, then he will have no choice to accept her decision and she would become dead to him. It's the only way he could go on living without her. That and one other way but he didn't want to think about the alternative.

Victor stepped out of the the hired black car and arranged for the driver to wait for his return. Forgetting he was dressed in his Halloween Clyde costume, Victor caught a glimpse of himself in the mirrored front doors of the office building. Finding his mirrored image humorous, Victor lips wore a large smirk. He entered the building hoping his encounter with Camden would be something of a misunderstanding. Victor was hopeful for a positive outcome but braced for worst. Even if the worst happened, he knew there was always an upside to a negative ending. He had a whole life ahead of him. Victor had a striving career, an enormous bank account and he would surely meet someone else, maybe even have kids someday. It was a strange way to look at things considering the worst hadn't even happened…yet. He had to remain positive for his own sanity; if not for himself but also for Mary. Victor's emotional rollercoaster was dragging him down, and quickly. He wasn't ready to let Mary go but he knew it was a good possibility that he may have no other choice with the matter. After his encounter with Camden, he was sure to have a path to follow whether he wanted to or not. He pictured a fist fight breaking out after a heated encounter; one good upper cut to the jaw would be enough to knock the bastard out. Knowing how much Mary despised confrontation, Victor envisioned her jumping in the middle of the quarrelling duo and getting sucker punched. He never wanted to hurt Mary, not even by accident.

Victor walked up to the group of men standing in the lobby and proceeded to shake each one of their hands. Grateful for their attendance, although they were being paid to be there, Victor drilled each of them with a series of instructions. Alessandro was the tallest of them all, also the ring leader of the group. His outgoing personality and social skills proved to be a great asset adding to his great people skills. His innate ability to read people without having to speak to them directly was a hidden talent that always worked to his advantage. Although he was strong and physically fit, his need for attention often made him stand out in a crowd. Most people were convinced his height was the reason for his noticeable presence but anyone who knew him personally got to experience his enthusiasm for life and revealing personality that made him the star of the crowd. He was pleasing to the eye for most women but the men who took notice where oddly aware of how comfortable he was in unfamiliar situations. For that reason alone, it made him an excellent private investigator. No one suspected his choice of career; in fact most people thought he was a business man of sorts. Alessandro filled Victor in on his team's new findings including the fact that Mary had arrived just as Victor had expected her to.

~28~

Mary hung onto the door handle to suite 704 for what felt like an eternity. She knew what she had come to do but finding the courage to do it was another story in itself. The door handle was well tattered and worn; used by so many people, indicative to the many people who passed through that very same doorway. She turned the knob to enter the office space remembering her purpose for her arrival. Inside was surprisingly bright with large floor to ceiling windows that spanned the entire east side of the open room. The air felt fresh and crisp with a faint aroma of cinnamon spice lingering through the space. The waiting area was lined with plush black leather chairs accompanied by stacks of previously read magazines. Small jack-o-lanterns were strategically placed around the room offering a festive look. The smell of fresh brewed coffee emanated from the open doorway to the left of the entrance. Mary walked in further to discover a large dark mahogany reception desk sporting a rather large pumpkin on the outer corner.

Victor's love for Halloween rang into her thoughts the moment she saw the carved pumpkin. His love of the holiday was charming and equally foolish, especially when he insisted they dress in outlandish costumes. As she approached the desk, she stared at the woman who sat behind it.

"Can I help you?" the receptionist questioned in a quivering tone. It was apparent the receptionist was startled by Mary's entrance into the office. The reception was deeply preoccupied with her work; she never took notice to Mary's initial arrival. It was an honest oversight as there were no scheduled appointments to attend to that day. Gwen was playing catch up at the office while Doctor Copeland attended to an important matter of his own behind the closed door of his private office.

"Don't I know you? I mean you look familiar to me," Mary responded not really answering the receptionist's question.

"I don't think so," she quickly replied. "I have one of those familiar faces. I get that question all the time."

"I'm here to see Doctor Copeland," Mary tells her.

Sounding nervous and unsure how to proceed, Gwen shuffled some paperwork around on her desk keeping her face out of Mary's direct sight.

"What did you say your name was?" Gwen asked trying hard to come up with a reasonable but believable reason to get Mary to leave.

"Mary. Mary Templemead," she answered.

Gwen could feel herself start to sweat. She thought about lying by telling Mary that Doctor Copeland wasn't in the office but that escape plan deflated the minute the Doctor let out a loud sneeze from inside his office. She then thought about coming up with a story of how multiple doctors' share their office space in order to keep fixed cost to a minimum but then Gwen realized Doctor Copeland's name was clearly the only one boldly marked on the door. Gwen's final lie came out of her mouth with great ease, which turned out not to be a lie at all.

"Do you have an appointment? I can't seem to find your name on my list of appointments," Gwen revealed without a stutter of pause.

Just before Mary could answer and respectfully start explaining her reason for the unscheduled visit, the door to the doctor's office opened. Gwen and Mary wore the same facial expression that consisted of confusion and panic, both for very different reasons.

Gwen jumped up from behind her desk and moved toward Doctor Copeland as if to create a human barrier of sorts. Gwen possessed a naturally ability to be creative. She was resourceful and intellectually quick giving her the upper hand in the most challenging situations. Planning to have Mary standing in her office was not a situation she thought would happen.

Mary's confusion radiated through her eyes, a look Doctor Copeland had witnessed before. She looked so troubled and so worried, a feeling the doctor painfully knew himself. No one said a word. They had no choice but to absorb the overwhelming streams of strong feelings floating within the four walls that surrounded them.

"Camden!" Mary finally spoke breaking the silence. "I didn't know you were a patient of Doctor Copeland's too?"

At the exact moment, Gwen and Camden took a good look at each other knowing that the truth they shared was still very much safe. It was only apparent to Camden that his lies lived a double life. The story he told to Gwen was a far different truth he still needed to tell Mary. The built up years of animosity and anguish were going to finally get released and to Camden it would all be worth it. His life, his dreams and his career meant nothing without his wife Adrianna at his side. He was prepared to lose it all.

"We need to talk Mary, please come into the office so we can have a private conversation,"

Camden softly spoke while gesturing her to enter his office. "Gwen, please hold all my calls for the rest of the day."

"Hold your calls? Camden? You're Doctor Copeland?" Mary started to put all the pieces together but not before she realized Camden had locked the door behind her. She could feel her heart beat speed up. Her years of hard business deals taught her to remain calm during stressful meetings but this type of stress was more than she could handle.

"Why did you feel the need to lie to me?" she asked.

Camden looked so broken and defeated; it almost made Mary feel bad for him. Perhaps that was the reaction he wanted from her.

"First let me get us some water before I begin to tell you the reason why I didn't let you know my true identity from the start," he asserted.

Camden made his way over to the small buffet servitor that was tucked to the side of his office. The fresh jug of water looked like it was newly prepared with the slices of lemon and lime floating on the water's surface. The crystal carafe had already formed a thin layer of moist condensation. Mary watched as the tiny drops of water rolled down the clear glass and land on the silver tray it sat on. The water looked refreshingly cold as Camden poured the fluid into the waiting glasses. Thinking Camden was too busy to notice, Mary pulled out her cell phone as a last minute attempt to text Victor.

"Please give me the dignity to explain myself before rushing off to call Victor," he pleaded without turning to look at Mary.

Mary was baffled on how Camden knew what she was doing, especially because his back was turned and there was no visible reflection from where she stood. Camden's tall and rather erect posture kept her from seeing what he was doing but the trickling sound of the splashing water falling into the glass indicated he was almost finished pouring. Her dry mouth turned into a pasty orifice crying out in thirst with every passing moment. Camden turned his attention back to her the moment he was done preparing their refreshments.

"I know you feel afraid of me right now, and rightfully so because I lied to you," he admitted walking up to her, placing the tall glass of water in her hand. The liquid was slightly foggy which Mary presumed was from the citrus clouding the water. She watched as the slice of lemon circled around and around in her water glass. Mary took the smallest sip from her glass just to show Camden that she trusted him. Her inner voice screamed otherwise but Mary knew she couldn't let her fear show. The water was cold, refreshing and untarnished of foul taste. Taking a larger drink before placing the glass on Camden's wooden desk Mary spoke frankly hoping to find answers to the many questions she had.

"I'm sure there is a reasonable explanation as to why you felt the need to withhold the truth from me," she lied. "You will have ample time to explain that to me but first I need to clear a few things up of my own. I am going back to New York in a few hours. I booked my flight already and I have a car service scheduled to pick me up directly from your office and take me straight to the airport. If you think you can talk me out of it this time, you are wrong. I know where I need to be and I am more sure about that now, more so than ever before in my life." Mary paused as if to collect more of her thoughts. Steering away from the reason as to why Camden lied to her in the first place. She brought the conversation back to them and their friendship. "I enjoyed our friendship. You opened up to me about your wife and how she passed. You allowed yourself to be vulnerable and that really opened up my eyes to the type of person you are. You are caring, sensitive, thoughtful and genuinely loving; so why the lie?"

"I have thought about this a great deal too. Don't think I enjoyed lying to you all these weeks," Camden started to explain the best way he knew how. Some of the words he spoke gave life to the truth but only to a certain extent. His plan had always been to take Victor's happiness away from him, just as Victor had done to him all those years ago. Camden never realized how difficult his planned task would be once he met Mary.

"Yes, but you did lie to me. I thought we were friends? How can you stand directly in front of me and continue to lie to my face?" Mary said with tears forming in eyes.

"I'm not lying to you right now Mary. It's your husband Victor that constantly lies to you. Maybe you should ask him why he hired me to become your friend. Maybe you should confront him on why he doesn't trust you to be in Toronto on your own? Maybe you…" as the words dropped from his tongue onto Mary's lap, Camden could see her disposition softening up toward him again. He knew placing doubt toward Victor's actions would break Mary's guard down and allow Camden room to build trust with her again. "I never wanted to hurt you."

"Well you failed in that department," Mary bitterly snapped feeling betrayed by both Camden and Victor.

"Being your friend started off as a job but it developed into so much more. I feel a real connection with you. You remind me so much of Adrianna that it actually hurts to walk away from you sometimes. Your charisma for life, your laughter and even your desire to be the strongest person possible reminds me of all the beautiful characteristics Adrianna held. You made it so easy and comfortable for me to talk to you and… well I don't have anyone else I can turn to," he explained pouring on more of a sympathy twist than honesty. He wanted to tell her the real reason for why he agreed to watch over her only he couldn't bring himself to saying the words out loud. There were no delicate words on how to describe to someone that you planned on killing them. How revenge was the only option to try and ease the deep pain and hurt that continued to ache in your soul.

"Hello? Are you still with me here?" Mary said sharply snapping Camden back into the current conversation. "Is that the only reason why you agreed to watch over me…because the great and powerful Victor is paying you to?"

Her words resonated deep within Camden, activating part of his inner malevolence. Mary was not expecting Camden to react the way he did. She watched as he moved his chair directly beside her and sat down leaving only a few inches of space between them. She could feel his body heat resonating from his pores. His breathing became desperate and shallow; his pupils were growing fully dilated in his blood shot eyes. Mary grew increasingly nervous with each one of his breaths that brushed across her face. She was slightly light headed almost faint but knew better not to move. She couldn't help but keep her stare directed in his eyes. Looking elsewhere would have indicated her fear of him and she knew he would be able to sense it like a rabid dog.

"I like talking to you," Mary lied hoping she could keep the situation calm.

"I like speaking to you too," Camden replied allowing the shallow words to seep through his clenched teeth.

"I like to meditate too, just like you directed me to. It really helped clear my head and allowed me to think with clear thoughts," Mary expelled hoping Camden would agree.

"Listen up you little pompous, spoiled, rich bitch! I am at my wits end with all this small talk. It's clear that you think Victor is the almighty one that you need to rush home to and have your perfect little life with while I rot in my own little hell. I have suffered the biggest loss of life when when I lost my wife and unborn child in that car accident that your husband caused." Camden's words haunted Mary's ears echoing vile and hateful lies. She didn't want to believe what he was saying but Mary knew Victor was in a terrible car accident years ago. Every once and a while he experienced flair ups from his accident injury. She couldn't keep her train of thoughts together. The room around her started spinning. Her dizzy state only worsened as she drank more water to ease her increasingly dry mouth.

"I don't understand…I'm feeling all fuzzy…did you…" Mary slumped back into her chair. Clenching onto her belly, she felt useless in protecting her unborn child. Although still conscious, Mary couldn't find the strength to get up and leave his office. She watched as he bent over her almost sniffing at her face. She could see the skin around his neck was flush and sweaty. She prayed, repeating the Our Father prayer and the Hail Mary silently in her head. Mary was certain her end was nearing, at the hands of a psychopath that she allowed into her life. Desperate to get her stomach to stop aching, she managed to shift onto her left side easing the growing pain ever so slightly. Leaning on her left side allowed her to get a better look at Camden's position which happened to be behind his desk. He was rifling through the left drawer throwing loose papers and rubbish by the handfuls onto the floor beside him. He appeared to be content as soon as he found what he was looking for. Unlucky for Mary, the gun he was holding was pointed directly at her. The word hate tattooed across his fingers clearly visible. She closed her eyes and waited for her final moment in time.

~29~

The loud bang resonated through the office. Gwen was shouting for Victor to leave but he was never one to back away from protecting the one he loved. Camden was equally startled with the loud crash when Victor kicked open the door to the locked office. Victor never expected to find Camden holding a gun to Mary however the unpredictable situation didn't stop him from approaching. Still dressed in his Clyde Halloween costume, Victor drew his fake hand gun out of his waist band and pointed it directly at Camden. It was his only option to try and defend himself.

"Drop your weapon…I have back up coming," Victor shouted in a strong and forceful tone. "You don't know what you're doing man!"

"I know exactly what I'm doing…man!" Camden retorted in a sarcastic manner.

"Let's talk about this calmly, like mature grown men," Victor said while lowering his fake pistol, now trying to reason with his words.

"I can't think straight. I'm falling apart. I don't know what to do anymore," Camden admitted still pointing the gun, but this time at Victor.

With a steady reach, Victor extended his hand out to Camden signaling him to hand over the weapon. Inching his way toward Mary, Victor needed to make sure she was okay. Her limp body and flaccid posture was not a good indication of her wellbeing.

"She's fine," Camden spoke up when he noticed Victor's attention was solely on Mary. "I gave her Rohypnol. Don't worry, she's had it before, she won't remember a thing when she wakes up."

"You gave her what? Okay…okay…okay," Victor repeated trying to gather his thoughts before his next move. "I'm going to walk over to her slowly and check on her, alright?" Victor asked not wanting to aggravate Camden more than he already was.

"You're not going near her!" he shouted. "Not before we get a few things straight."

"Listen to me Camden," Victor uttered trying to take control of the situation. "We're friends. We've been friends for many, many years. You're one of the guys I've always looked up to. You're smart and enthusiastic about everything, always soaring above and beyond anyone's expectations.

This isn't you," Victor continued to say while pointing at Mary still unconscious in the chair.

"It's who I've become ever since you killed my wife and unborn child. I changed the night you took them away from me. You stole my entire world, my worth, everything that ever mattered to me right from under my feet. You did this to me…you!" Camden bellowed out through a thick build up of slobber and spit. Victor could see Camden's rage escalating with every attempt he made to justify his change in behaviour.

"I don't understand how I did this to you? Please help me understand so I can make it right again," Victor pleaded as he watched his friend continue to break down.

"Don't pretend you don't know what I'm talking about. I'm sure you remember the accident you caused that night in Barrie…when you ran my wife's car off the road," Camden started to explain. "With all those years in the courtroom combined with your exuberant ability to remember every last detail about a case that grants you a win in court over and over again and you're trying to convince me that you don't remember a car accident? Excuse me, not just an accident but an accident that killed three people and seriously injuring one other?

"Yes, I was involved in an accident...in Barrie but I had no idea that was your wife," Victor confessed with visible sadness emanating from deep within his core. "You have to believe that it was an accident Camden. An unfortunate accident that I wished never happened, more so now than ever."

"Oh, you wish it never happened do you?" Camden childishly repeated as if mocking Victor's remorse would help the situation. "I bet it keeps you up all night long as you lay beside that beautiful wife of yours; all cozy and comfortable, making plans for the future. The future I will never have with my wife and child. The future you took from me."

Victor watched as Camden stood beside Mary, stroking the hair off of her face. He observed Camden's gentle touch smooth away the last strand that lay across her cheek bone. Victor knew how close they must have gotten over the past few weeks but he never guessed Camden would hold such an obsession for her. Victor was sure there was some form of unspoken intimacy between them based on the text pictures Camden strategically sent. It was frightening to know how unstable Camden had become after all of their years of friendship. What he found more troubling was that he didn't do any kind of background check before eagerly placing Mary into Camden's unbalanced care.

"I know you're hurting, I'm hurting for you too. Please let me help you before you do something that affects the rest of your life," Victor pleaded hoping Camden would snap out of his psychosis.

"Help me?" Camden mocked again, laughing and waving his handgun around carelessly. "Like the way you helped me on that fateful fall day when you decided to drive erratically? You are the one who caused my wife's car to swerve off the road. Oh…that night Adrianna fought for her life, desperately trying to survive for our baby's sake." Camden's sarcasm quickly turned back to sorrow. "I'll be just fine. You don't need to worry about me. You see, I bought this gun a short while ago seriously thinking about offing myself. You know like blowing my brains right out the back of my head, just like this."

Camden's volatile behaviour was worsening by the moment as he placed the handgun under his chin. Victor never planned on this type of confrontation with Camden. He was thankful that he pre-arranged back up with the private investigators that were eagerly waiting downstairs. Close to fifteen minutes had passed, just the right amount of time to set the group of private investigators in motion. Unsure of what

Victor might have encountered, he instructed the men to meet him in Doctor Copeland's office, but only if he hadn't returned within a half hour. With only fifteen minutes to spare, Victor knew his altercation with Camden was limited. He just hoped he could hold him off long enough.

"See man, this is exactly what I'm talking about. You don't want to do that! Think about Mary and how disappointed she would be," Victor softly spoke hoping his words would deflect the emotions Camden had for Mary and help redirect his threatening actions. "It's obvious the two of you forged a strong friendship. I'm sure you've both helped each other out a great deal. Still talking, Victor approached Camden holding his hands up in a peaceful manner indicating that he wanted no harm. "Please Buddy, just put the gun away."

Camden took a step back from Mary's chair and slowly lowered the handgun to his side. They both watched as Mary struggled to wake from her unconscious state. Still weak and unsure as to what was happening, she blinked repeatedly eager to see past her foggy vision.

"Oh thank God you're here… she said in a tender breath. Mary was relieved to see Victor standing beside her. For the first time in her life she was happy to have him rescue her. She couldn't come up with one single reason to give him trouble for his need to protect her. It was then, at that very moment that she needed him the most.

Victor reached down and placed his hand on her shoulder giving Mary notice that he was right beside her and that everything would be okay.

"It's not about anyone else right now, can't you see? It's about me! My hurt! My loss! My wife! My baby! Everything you have now should be mine, including your baby," Camden blurted out.

"Baby?" Victor questioned. "What baby?"

Fully conscious but still groggy, Mary looked up at Victor while stroking her belly tenderly nodding her head up and down indicating truth to Camden's words.

"It's true," she verbally confirmed. "We're pregnant. I just found out today we are expecting a baby."

Unable to control his excitement, Victor threw his arms around her.

"I was so worried about you here in Toronto, all by yourself," he explained to her forgetting about Camden still standing in the room. "I hired Camden to watch over you…I never knew he was…

"You never knew he was all what Victor?" Camden spoke up aiming his caulked gun at both

Victor and Mary. "You never knew I would have such an astounding affect on your lovely wife? You never knew your devoted wife could fall for a guy like me?"

"That's enough!" Victor yelled taking a step closer to Camden. His hurtful words rang through Victor's ears leaving him shaking with rage. "Not one more word about my wife, you hear me?"

"Oh Victor, did I upset you?" Camden taunted. "Please, excuse me for my lack of manners. Maybe I should let Mary explain how she accidently fell into my arms one night after dinner and drinks. How she confided in me that you are a lousy husband who never gives her the benefit of the doubt. How overprotective you are and…"

As Victor listened to Camden's twisted version of events, he couldn't help wonder if some of what he was saying rang a bit of truth. Did Mary really feel that way? Was that the reason she needed to get away?

"Victor, please don't listen to him. He's obviously trying to push your buttons. I'm sorry he's saying all these spiteful things," Mary declared while apologizing for Camden's crazy talk. "Is that really your translation of our friendship Camden?"

"Our friendship?...ya…sure! Is that how you're going to spin it to your husband Mary? "I love you…Mary," he whispered. Camden no longer looked like a professional doctor, but rather a broken man who was in some serious need of mental help. His expression of love toward Mary exposed his gentleness and kindness as he reached out to touch her arm. "Mary, don't you remember that night we shared together? Your magical fingers caressed my body sending shivers down to my toes. You let me explore your body as you lay in my arms, letting out a soft moan whenever I stroked your inner thigh. Remember? I told you how much I wanted you ever since the day I met you. We had so much fun at night. We talked, we laughed and we drank."

"Camden, that never happened!" Mary bellowed out terrified Victor would believe the lies he so easily spoke.

"I never knew I could feel that way about another woman before. Not after Adrianna passed did I ever think I could fall in love again. It was never my plan to love you like I do. That is why it's so difficult," Camden said trying to explain his actions to Mary. "You weren't supposed to be so caring and understanding. I wasn't supposed to fall in love with you, but it didn't matter because either way I would get to take you away from

Victor just like he took Adrianna away from me. Only Adrianna is dead and can never come back to me. This is why you can't go back to Victor, not after all that we've shared. Not after discovering he killed my wife and child."

"Camden, please listen to me," Mary guided with her soft spoken words. "I'm going to stay with you for as long as it takes to get you the help you need, but I'm not in love with you. You need to know that your feelings toward me are misguided because of the hurt you're suffering. More importantly, you need to come to terms with Adrianna's death. It wasn't Victor who killed her. It was the limo driver who carelessly checked his text messages while driving."

Mary got up from her chair for the first time since the toxic drug wore off, her legs still wobbly but sturdy enough to hold the weight of her thin build. Taking her first few steps toward Camden, Mary kept her arms open in an attempt to give him a hug. Although his hurtful banter about them having an affair was cruel and uncalled for, she couldn't stand watching his pain unfold in front of her eyes. She just wanted to console his hurt and pain, help the ache and loneliness go away even for just a short while.

Gwen tirelessly tried to keep the group of private investigators from barging into Camden's office.

Victor could hear her shouting that Doctor Copeland was in a private meeting. It only took a moment before chaos broke out. There was shouting and pushing. Gwen was shaking while she attempted to call for security.

Without notice, the piercing sound of a gunshot rang loud through the office. More panic, screams and crying where heard from everyone. Camden fell back, hitting the floor hard, shocked at what happened. Mary's body lay flat, face down on the floor situated between Camden and Victor. Victor fell on his knees unable to keep his legs from holding him upright. Trying hard to stop the blood from pouring out of the gaping hole in Mary's chest, Victor pressed firmly against the gunshot wound hoping to slow her blood loss.

"Call an ambulance!" Victor shouted to anyone who would listen. "I'm losing her, I'm losing her quickly. Hurry, please hurry."

Victor robotically started chest compressions on Mary. He watched as her chest gurgled with bubbles of bloodied air with each compression he made. He was not going to give up. He knew he had to keep working on her until the paramedics arrived. It would be the only way to save her and his baby. His exhausted frame kept hovered over her, tirelessly pumping her chest in hopes that it would be enough to keep her heart from stopping.

"I love you more than I can ever tell you," he whispered into her ear as he checked for a pulse. He desperately wished she would say it back to him one more time, but she never did. He watched as she slipped away.

~30~

Five long agonizing years passed without Mary by his side and Victor loathed ever waking moment of them. He was never able to look at her picture without crying but even through his tears he remembered all of their good times together. Every Halloween he would pull her picture out of his wallet and stare hopelessly at it. This year was no different. After admiring her beauty through his constant stream of tears, Victor placed her picture upright onto his dresser. Although he knew she was not with him anymore, he often felt her presence. Today he found it extra hard to be without her. The pain of her absence was too strong to ignore. Not only did Halloween mark the anniversary of Mary's death but it was also a holiday Victor once looked forward to celebrating. Alone in his room where he and Mary once shared their hopes and dreams, Victor sat and contemplated whether or not he could continue to chair the Gala for the Homeless and Hungry. The charity was founded so both he and Mary could help bring a better life to some of the less fortunate people in their community. How could he continue to help others when he was struggling to help himself? Sure he could throw a wad of money into the Gala and dish out verbal support to others without even blinking but deep inside Victor just didn't have the strength to fake his happiness anymore. He couldn't show up at one more Gala dressed in the year's choice of costume and ramble on about how the charity was founded. He had lost his passion for Halloween, it died the same day Mary did. The past four years of hosting the Gala without her always ended up with Victor coming back to his penthouse completely annihilated. He didn't want to feel anymore, desperate to numb his pain. Getting drunk was the only thing he could do to keep himself from emotionally falling apart in front of his Gala guests.

He remembered her gentle touch and the sweet sound of her tender voice. Sometimes he talked to her picture, telling her how hard it was to live without her. He imagined Mary gently laying her arms around his neck and reassuring him that everything would be okay and that one day they would be reunited. He openly promised her that he would never forget the joy and love she brought to his life and that one day they would hold each other again.

Sometimes he pictured what their baby would have looked like. He was almost positive he or she would have had dark hair and a radiant smile that stretched across their angelic face. He knew Mary's beauty would radiate through their little soul, for Mary had the purest of souls one could have ever had. Victor envisioned walking through Soho hand in hand with his little one, eager to show them bits and pieces of the neighbourhood that only a true nature lover would appreciate. He would watch as his child ran through the grassy laneway over to the hidden playground enthusiastically waiting to be pushed on the swings.

Victor could image the endless nights he would rush home from work just to be able to get his child to their soccer game on time or maybe it would be karate. Whatever their child wanted to participate in, Victor would be happy to oblige. He pictured his vibrant wife prancing around joyfully snapping pictures of everything, wanting to capture every little detail of their child growing up. Every thought of what could have been had Victor mourning that much more.

He thought about reaching out to his grief support group, like he's done so many times before but this time he couldn't find it in him to listen to another story of how important it was to live life after the loss of a loved one. He had been doing that for five years already and the pain never dimmed. Although he did find companionship with Norah through attending group meetings, she was never able to draw him out of his depression. Norah suffered a similar loss when her husband passed away the year prior. She would tell Victor how much he was helping her to cope with her loss. Although he was sympathetic to her, he didn't want the burden of helping someone else with their pain management. Not when he couldn't manage his own pain. He only wanted to concentrate on getting his own pain to leave. The constant and relentless ache of losing his wife was too much for him to take. Mary was the only woman he shared a deep seeded love for. She was a devoted wife who believed in helping others without wanting anything in return. She didn't deserve to die the way she did. There was still so much for her to accomplish. She was just supposed to be sorting out some unresolved issues from her past. A past she worked hard to leave behind so she could move onto her future. A future she was going to have with Victor and their baby. She had so much more life to live.

Over the years, Victor held onto so much guilt. His inner guilt of pushing Mary to seek treatment haunted him the most. Threatening to leave her so she would seek treatment was a constant reminder of his ignorance that replayed in his head. The guilt of agreeing with Mary to go to Toronto on her own stood a close second to his invariable torture. The unforgivable guilt of hiring Camden to watch over his beloved wife was what haunted his dreams every night. Victor emotionally punished himself over and over but that punishment was never going to bring Mary back to him. Blindly handing Mary over to Camden without first seeking a personal background check hurt Victor the most. Mary would still be alive and in his arms if he did his research like he always had in the past. Those closing thoughts helped Victor realize his life would never be the same. Not just because of his loss, but because he would never forgive himself for his own thoughtless and selfish behaviour. Victor closed his eyes and tried hard to think of only the great moments he shared with Mary. Starting from their wedding day when she walked toward him in her simple, but flowing wedding gown. The smile on her face glowed more than the hundreds of lit candles that lined the church altar. Not wanting to make a big fuss about her day, Mary kept her hairstyle simple wearing it down with just a decorative pin holding her bangs to the side; keeping them from sliding over her eyes. Her A-line lace dress draped her petit frame perfectly offering excellent precision to its no waist seams. Mary floated down the aisle effortlessly as if she had walked those steps a million times before. She was a natural beauty, a trait she never abused.

Their honeymoon in Maui was nothing short of spectacular. They spent endless hours exploring each other making careful mental notes of each other's likes and dislikes. It was that trip when Victor discovered Mary's fault line with trust. For every time Victor attempted to explore deeper into their intimacy, Mary retracted and shut herself down. He never regretted their raw moments. It was those moments that allowed an open dialogue to happen between them. It was those types of moments that helped Victor understand Mary's unwillingness to fully open up to him. Victor was able to get a glance at how deeply scared she was as a result of her past relationship. He experienced firsthand the pain she suffered as he watched her curled up in a ball crying uncontrollably. Their honeymoon may not have been traditional in the sense of lover's paradise but it was a honeymoon that gave him more than he ever imagined it to. It was a honeymoon of opportunity. Victor was grateful for the opportunity. It allowed him to connect with his wife on a whole new personal level. A connection he cherished more than hours of love making or fine dining could ever offer.

The talk of having children came within a few years of their vows. Building a solid career was always their plan before adding to their family. A decision and plan they were both in agreeance with. He wanted nothing more than to become a father to a beautiful baby girl. He hoped she would inherit her mother's striking looks but more importantly Mary's charisma and zest for life. Mary was a people pleaser; always putting other people's needs in front of her own. Perhaps that was her greatest downfall but it was just one more quality she possessed that Victor loved.

Every year that passed without Mary in his life, Victor grew more lonely and desolate. Nothing mattered to him much anymore. His passion for his law practice dissipated; slowly diminishing the goodwill of his firm. He didn't care. Victor would spend days at home, by himself without even opening the blinds for sunlight. Today was no different. His support group told him that his pain and hurt would subside with time, but he hasn't been lucky enough to experience that. It's been five years and his pain has not dulled. A colleague suggested he go on a few dates in order to allow himself the chance to meet other people, but no one could ever replace his love for Mary. The few dates he did attempt with Norah only refreshed the notion that they both suffer the same type of loss. There should have been some comfort in that but Victor couldn't find it. He didn't feel the connection with her, he wanted his connection with Mary and that was all he could think of. The disconnect Victor felt with the world was always more powerful than the healing process.

Victor sat up and took the picture of Mary into his hands. Resting back onto his bed, he kissed her picture and placed it face down on his chest; right where he thought she could feel his heart beating the strongest. Victor knew it would be a matter of minutes before he slipped into an unconscious state. He could already feel the effects of the Oxycontin he ingested earlier. The empty pill bottle still lay on the bed next to him. There was no coming back from Victor's sleepy trance. He had made up his mind the moment he swallowed all the pills from the bottle. With the pills now slowing his respiratory system, Victor knew it would only be moments before he would be reunited with Mary. There was no need to be the strong one anymore. All the times he hid the pain he felt, the torment he endured watching her suffer, the sorrow he buried deep inside; careful not to let it show on his surface. Victor was the one who mastered the true skill of hiding his feelings. He knew if he let his emotions pour out, he would be the one who was viewed as weak, unstable and maybe even vulnerable. Never wanting to be anything less than a strong man, Victor kept up his charade for the sake of Mary. Although Victor would tell Mary how much he loved and needed her, she never knew the extent to those words. Mary was his everything, his foundation of strength, his hopes and dreams, his reason to succeed, his everything; including the reason he breathed. They had nearly ten years together, and it was the best ten years of his life.

"I'm coming Mary," he whispered feeling his pain weaken with every slowing heartbeat until his heart stopped completely.

ABOUT THE AUTHOR

Joanne Vivolo was born on March 20 1974, the youngest of four siblings from Hamilton, Ontario.

After graduating with a degree in Business from Mohawk College, Joanne immediately started working in Radio. She eventually expanded her media horizon to include telecommunications and cable television. After starting a family, Joanne continued with her creative score and went on to write and publish fictional novels.

Her first novel ***Too Close to Almost*** was released near the end of 2014. Following the success of her first realistic fictional novel, she continued with her creative spirit and completed her first mature romance novel titled ***Protect Me Not.*** Joanne has been a full-time author and parent to three children since 2002.

With the likes of fellow Author Lea Black and TV Personality on The Real Housewives of Miami endorsing her work, Joanne is sure to continue to create some spectacular novels.

Other Books Written by Joanne Vivolo

Too Close To Almost

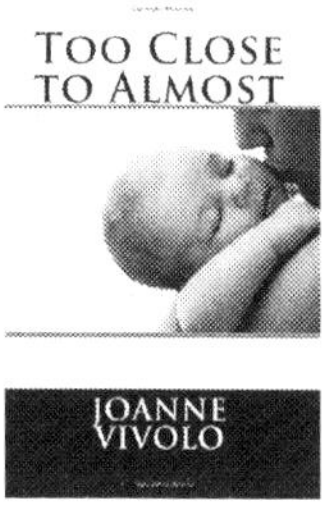

Join and Follow Joanne Vivolo on

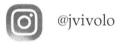

@jvivolo

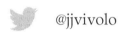

@jjvivolo

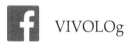

VIVOLOg

www.joannevivolo.com

61191657R00175

Made in the USA
Charleston, SC
17 September 2016